Restless Spirits

by

Maurice Holloway

https://mauriceholloway.wixsite.com/mauricehollowaybooks

Facebook: https://facebook.com/MauriceHollowayAuthor
Instagram: https://www.instagram.com/mauricehollowayauthor
Twitter: https://twitter.com/MFHAuthor

Haunted Houses

All houses wherein men have lived and died
Are haunted houses. Through the open doors
The harmless phantoms on their errands glide,
With feet that make no sound upon the floors.

We meet them at the door-way, on the stair,
Along the passages they come and go,
Impalpable impressions on the air,
A sense of something moving to and fro.

There are more guests at table than the hosts
Invited; the illuminated hall
Is thronged with quiet, inoffensive ghosts,
As silent as the pictures on the wall.

The stranger at my fireside cannot see
The forms I see, nor hear the sounds I hear;
He but perceives what is; while unto me
All that has been is visible and clear.

We have no title-deeds to house or lands;
Owners and occupants of earlier dates
From graves forgotten stretch their dusty hands,
And hold in mortmain still their old estates.

Henry Wadsworth Longfellow – 1807-1882

1

'We have to hold the hands,' Carla instructed, her 'have' sounding like 'haff'. 'It is compulsory for the séance.'

'Listen to her,' said Rogerson in his deep, cultured voice, 'she's from Transylvania; they know about these things.'

'What? Is she a vampire?' sneered Kingsley Nutball, baring his teeth.

'I don't like him,' I told Trinity as I peered into his piggy eyes. 'Sarcastic creep. He's just like that pompous Shadwick.'

Trinity went up to his face, staring at him left and right. 'It's true. Same eyes, same big nose,' she poked it, 'and with a white wig he'd look exactly like him.'

Nutball scratched his nose, looking puzzled. He couldn't see us, of course.

'Is there really somewhere called Transylvania?' Arathea chirruped in her Manchester accent. 'I thought it was fictitious, like Dracula.'

Carla stood and gasped, looking around as if to see if any immortals were listening. She smoothed her black dress; it was the only colour she ever wore, and sat.

I whispered to Trinity; I don't know why, no-one can hear us, 'You know why people don't like Dracula, don't you?'

'Because he bites?'

'Because he's a pain in the neck, ha, ha!'

Carla said, 'Transylvania is part of my country: Romania.'

When Carla first arrived, I had to ask Trinity where Romania was. She's educated, see; I'm only a footman.

'Between Hungary and the Black Sea,' she reminded me. 'Remember we used to study the maps in the library? When we had atlases.'

'And when we had a library.'

'Will you hold me please, Doctor Nutball,' Zinnia, Arathea's aunt reached for his soft hand careful not to injure him with her long, orange nails. With her garish, flowing chiffons she looked like she should be holding the meeting. 'I always feel safe with a professional man.'

Trinity muttered, 'Yes, well . . . , think we know why.'

I shushed her.

Carla took control. 'That is good, Mrs Zinnia;' her Z was an S, 'I take his other one. Now Miss Arathea, take your auntie's hand and your fiancé on the other side,' she nodded at Rogerson Lovatt, 'and I take this one. We start now and nobody do the silly things like kicking table or making the fun noises. Spirits are serious bus—'

Nutball interrupted. 'I'll say they are. My whisky glass is nearly empty. Can't have a good séance if you're sober. Ha!' He began to rise from his seat.

'Shut up, creep!' I said to him. He didn't hear. 'Creep, creep, creep!'

'Sit down, Kingsley,' his host commanded. 'Sometimes I find it hard to believe you're a magistrate; aren't you supposed to be open-minded?'

'Had any juicy cases lately, Kingsley?' asked Zinnia.

'Not really. The other day I had a family dispute that got out of hand, a young woman for repeated shoplifting, graffiti vandalism by an otherwise intelligent teenage boy – very artistic actually, and a near murder.'

'How can it be a "near murder"?' asked Arathea, a frown topping her green eyes.

'It was a fellow trying to explain why driving at eighty through a pedestrian precinct was acceptable as he was late for a meeting. It was a near murder because I felt like strangling him!'

Rogerson interrupted the narration. 'Back to the matter in hand. Let's go along with Carla. She's been here a month as housekeeper getting the place ready so if she says it's haunted, she knows better than us.' Rogerson smiled at Carla. 'And we all experienced the weird events of yesterday.'

'I like him,' Trinity whispered in a girly way, 'despite his grammar. It ought to be *better than we* not *us.*'

I looked across the table at Rogerson Lovatt, the man who'd rescued Ruddyard Park from the demolition men. For years Trinity and I believed the house would either fall down around us of its own accord or some navvies would turn up one day to knock it down. I had to admit it; Mr Lovatt was good-looking. And quite young for a rich man; in his thirties I guessed. Mind you, Mr Daniel was only that sort of age.

'You don't have to whisper. They can't hear us or see us, Trinity; we're ghosts. Anyway, you're engaged to Daniel Washbury. It even says so in that history book Shadwick, sorry Nutball, was reading.'

'Oh, Albie, do you think we'll ever see our loved ones again: my Daniel and your Lizzie?'

'It's the only way I keep going, Miss Trinity; by believing we will. Perhaps this nice Miss Carla can help, eh?'

Kingsley Nutball sat twirling his whisky tumbler and responded like a spoilt child. He looked at his host over the top of his glasses. 'OK, if you say so. But don't forget I'm a psychiatrist. Every day I deal with people who see and hear things that aren't there. Ghosts? Spirits? Pah! Maybe you can conjure up my distant relative. Apparently he used to work here as a butler about a hundred-and-fifty-years ago or something. Let me know if Jeremiah Shadwick calls in would you. Ha, ha, ha, ha!'

'See, see, see,' I shouted.

'You were right Albie! That's why he looks like him. That horrid butler used to look down his nose at me.'

'Well, if he does turn up after all this time, I'll certainly give him a piece of my mind even if it is a hundred-and-fifty-years late.' I pushed out my chest.

'Why haven't you said anything before?' asked Arathea.

'There's hardly been any time, has there, what with all the goings on. Anyway, I told Rogerson, didn't I?' Lovatt nodded agreement. 'From what I remember being told by my father,

4

Jeremiah was in service back in the late nineteenth century, like half the population in those days. Seemingly he worked at several big houses in the county, building himself up from boot boy to butler. Pretty well-paid number at that time.'

'So, he was what? Great-grandparent or something?'

'I can't recall now. It was on my dad's side several generations ago; there was a family tree somewhere which might still be in the old family papers.'

'I'd like to see that Kingsley,' said Rogerson. 'Anyway, let's get back to it. Carla?'

'You hold my hand, Kingsley,' said Zinnia, 'I scare easily.'

'Boo!' shouted Trinity which made me laugh. It had no effect on Zinnia.

The psychiatrist didn't hear us. He pushed his glasses to the top of his head and just droned on to the aunt; a captive audience of one. 'If there are any spirits here it'll probably be the two traitors. Story goes they got what was coming to them which is why they were left buried under the stable.'

Arathea put her hands to her pale cheeks. 'S-so it c-could be true. A haunted house?'

Rogerson patted her on the arm.

Trinity and I gawped at each other.

'Traitors! How dare he?'

'Got what was coming? We're innocent!'

'We'll prove it one day, won't we Trinity? If only I could find my letter.' I couldn't help myself. I whacked his spectacles which fell over his bald spot and slid off the back of his head. 'Take that creepy Shadwick!'

'What the . . . ? Was that you, Carla? You remember your place, madam.'

Trinity turned on me. 'Now see what you've done, Albert Hapless. You've got that poor lady into trouble.'

'Well, he deserved it. Traitors indeed. Hmph.'

'Look, she's got them settled ready to begin. Let's sit down and watch.'

'Do you think she'll call on us? W-what'll we say? I hope no other spirits turn up.'

'Why, Albie?'

'I was always frightened of ghosts.'

2

It must have been a couple of years ago; Trinity and I realised something was going on. People wearing white or yellow hard hats began arriving every day, walking around the house measuring floors and walls, poking sticks into the wood and plaster. All carrying tiny boxes with lights on them. Others went up on the roof using a contraption like a little cage to hoist them. Very clever. We hadn't seen anybody inside the house since the army people were here in 1945. Officially, that is. There was a group of youngsters once who broke in to hold a drinking party but we found a way of persuading them to leave. An army hospital, it was. For war wounded. They were good years. People dying all the time; we made lots of new friends. But then they all left when it closed; went on the trucks with all the live ones. That was seventy years or more since.

'That's it, Albie, I think they're preparing to pull the old place down.'

'What will we do? Where shall we live? This has been my home for . . . ,' I checked on my fingers, 'ten years alive and about a hundred-and-fifty as a ghost.'

'If they build another house we'll simply change bedrooms, I suppose.'

'But I like sleeping in the Master's bedroom.'

I saw a wistful look in her eye. 'Yes, so did I. Aaah,' she sighed.

'Miss Trinity Hope! I trust you're not saying what I think you're saying.'

'Oh. I-I, er . . . .' She twiddled strands of long black hair through her fingers. 'What do you mean, Albie?'

'I sincerely hope that a nice girl like you wasn't dancing a two-step with her fiancé before the band had started playing.'

'What?'

'Don't play innocent with me Miss Trinity, I've known you too long. You know what I mean. Trying out the controversial relations before the priest has blessed the amalgamation.'

'Are you suggesting sex with Daniel?'

'No! I am certainly not suggesting it – or recommending it!'

'It's a bit late now anyway. Didn't you and Lizzie . . . ?'

If I wasn't already seated I'd have had to sit down. 'Most certainly not! My Lizzie is as pure as a field of new snow.' I felt my cheeks getting redder than they normally were. I don't usually discuss such matters, certainly not with the masters or mistresses. 'Mind you, she wouldn't have been if that Jeremiah Shadwick'd had his way.'

'Don't worry. We'll find somewhere.'

'Well, only as long as it's on the estate. That preacher bound us here for all eternity.'

'Don't let's jump the fence too early. Let's see what happens here.'

Well now, what happened was, shortly after the measuring men came and went, dozens and dozens of builders arrived with scaffolding and ladders, trucks and machines. Everyone wore the same hats. Oh, the noise! But we were happy. They weren't knocking it down; it looked like they were rebuilding the old place. Or some of it, at least.

When I was a young boy, my parents used to take me to see stately homes like Blenheim and Chatsworth; huge properties impossible for a kid from a suburban semi-detached to imagine living in. I could never understand why a lady might want a bedroom the length of a cricket pitch. I used to prefer the mansions and manor houses; still grand living but at least the rooms were of realistic sizes.

On every trip my father's words rang in my ears, 'Now, remember Roger, son, no touching, my boy.'

I enjoyed feasting my eyes on the paintings, the suits of armour, the carved furniture and windows draped with enough fabric to make a velvet cover for ours and next door's house. But what I wanted more than anything in the world was to touch. I wanted to unhook the thick red rope from its brass pole and put my feet on the carpet that had come all the way from Persia by camel and boat to England then horse and cart hundreds of years earlier. I wanted to sit in a chair that was even older than both my grandparents and stroke the carved grooves and flowers. I longed to bounce on a bed stuffed with horsehair just to see how it compared to plastic foam and springs. I yearned for someone to put a sword in my hand so I could marvel at how the knights of old could swing it in battle. Always, the unwavering stare of the National

Trust lady or man sitting in the corner dared me with a look that said I'd be chained up in an instant. Other boys and girls of my age, strangers, would share similar thoughts. I overheard adults whispering, 'Wouldn't it be good if we could . . . .'

As I grew older I continued to visit those places and came to appreciate the amazing but difficult task taken on by the National Trust: acquiring, rebuilding, displaying and protecting some of the most beautiful heritage buildings in the world on behalf of the nation and the general public. Understandably, they didn't want their vintage artefacts destroyed by children's grubby fingers and gritty shoes.

I used to say to my dad, 'There must be a middle road; a compromise. Visitors demand access these days. To keep them coming back it must be fun as well as informative.'

'I agree, Roger, son, but it's expensive and the National Trust doesn't have unlimited funds.'

So, when I made my first billion, I knew what I wanted to do. I bought an abandoned sixteenth-century manor house in the Midlands, restored and furnished it before gifting it to the National Trust. There was one proviso. Everything must be accessible to visitors unless it presented a health and safety risk. Other than that, every chair could be sat on, tables leant on, carpets walked on, furnishings stroked. Best of all; four-poster beds could be lain on. And staff were to help people do it. It worked. My dad loves it!

My team and I learnt a lot from that exercise. Our second purchase was a similar building in East Anglia. The third was larger. So far, Ruddyard Park is the largest – and most expensive. Friends have said it's a lot of money to spend only to give away. My answer is always the same. In the last few years whilst I've donated millions, I've earned several billion pounds. Ridiculous, I know but there it is. It's a beautiful house which visitors will adore.

I was sitting in the kitchen one day where it's cool, imagining the smell of Mrs Carter's pies baking. Upstairs was noisier than one of those northern manufactories I once visited; banging, sawing, hammering in every bedroom. Trinity floated down through the ceiling waving her arms in excitement like a maddened housefly.

'Come upstairs. See what I've found. Quickly before they move it.'

I can't do floors and ceiling like she can. Maybe it's a woman thing, you know how they have this habit of appearing from nowhere. I can only do sideways so walls and doors aren't a problem for walking through but I can't do uppy-downy like Trinity. I went up the stairs to meet her in the dining room. She was standing by a table on which sheets of paper had been unrolled.

'Look. Recognise it?'

It was a drawing of the old dining room as it had been created by Lady Margaret Kingswood, my first employer. And Lizzie's.

'I remember when her ladyship commissioned the artist to do this.

'After his lordship passed away, Lady Margaret decided to brighten her home from the dark and dingy place it was under Sir George. She invited furniture makers and drapery merchants to visit from Buckinghamshire, carpet men from Axminster, designers from London. It was rumoured she spent more than two hundred pounds. The house sparkled with new paint, beeswax and bright satins. Even us male staff had new pale-blue uniforms. So proud was her ladyship she wanted the results recorded.

'The artist, a man with a German-sounding name, stayed in the servants' quarters for about a month. He wasn't an old chap, perhaps in his late-twenties. He had a liking for English ale which he told us was "werry vunderbar" as he quaffed several each evening in the servants' hall. We laughed at the way he mixed his Vs and Ws. His paintings were really accurate – despite all the beer.'

'*We* staff, Albie, not *us* staff. It's exactly as it was when Daniel bought the house. Oh, the wonderful dinner parties we used to have in this room. Do you recall them, Albie?'

'Yes, I used to serve you, *Miss* Trinity. You always drank too much wine, I thought.'

'I know. You used to quietly caution me if I became too garrulous. My guardian angel.'

'Then and now.'

I'd forgotten all about the workmen in the room. One of them came over to the table, walking right through me. I hate it when that happens; makes me go all hot and dizzy. I staggered, knocking a large cup onto the floor before Trinity could steady me. Many years ago, we discovered we could move small objects.

When you first become a ghost, it takes a bit of getting used to: like walking through things or people, for example, or having live people walk through you. And people not knowing you're there cos they can't see or hear you. I think there're different categories because some of the dead soldiers we met could be seen by their old mates. Unlike me and Trinity, however. they couldn't move things about which is why it was possible for me to knock over his cup. Oddly though, I could walk through his table with the cup on top and have no effect. It's something to do with the amount of effort, Trinity said. I'm glad we can touch some things because in our early years we were able to read every book in the library; thousands of them. And we'd already had a bit of fun earlier at everyone's expense which is one of the main reasons they agreed to Carla's seance.

'Oy, careful mate!' called another man. 'Don't you damage them paintings.'

'*Those* paintings,' Trinity corrected him.

He retrieved his cup, unbroken. ''S alright. Keep your drawers on.'

I quickly put my hands over Trinity's ears.

Trinity moved them. 'Don't worry, Albie, I know what drawers are. I do wear them.'

This time I covered my ears whilst singing one of my favourite tunes:

He'd fly through the air with the greatest of ease,

That daring young man on the flying trapeze.

La,la – la,la,la, de, da-da-da, dum.

When I saw her mouth stop moving I said, 'That is not a subject a delicate young lady should discuss with a gentleman even if he is only a footman.'

To emphasise my position, I tugged on the points of what remained of my pale-blue uniform waistcoat, grubby after the stable wall fell on us. Two brass buttons were missing; at the bottom of the ditch presumably, along with one of my silver shoe buckles. I can't imagine what Lady Margaret would have said if she could see me now with torn breeches and my silk hose in tatters. I used to pride myself on my appearance but there's nothing I can do about it.

Mind you, Trinity didn't look much better. Her beautiful gold-coloured velvet gown was missing a sleeve; the remaining one had lost its lace trim. The grubby skirt was ripped from the hem to the knee displaying a shocking amount of ankle and leg.

'I don't feel like a delicate young anything!' said Trinity. 'Anyway, do you see what they're doing?'

'Making a mess, you mean?'

'No. Look at the colours on the wall there,' she pointed, 'and see what that man is doing to the columns? These men are re-creating our old home, Albie.'

'You're right. Exactly as it was.'

'And,' she turned over the sheet, 'they've got drawings of all the rooms in the house.'

'So, do you think they're going to . . . .'

'Yes. The whole house will come alive again. How exciting!'

'That'll cost a few hundred, I'll wager.'

3

So, there we were two years later sitting in the drawing room. What I saw was exactly what I would have seen if I'd blinked a hundred-and-fifty-years ago when I opened my eyes again. It was as if all our ghostly years had never been.

The walls were the same colour; the pale green of new leaves in the spring with a darker diamond pattern. I'd searched every inch of that room looking for Lizzie's letter after those criminals had been in there. The marble fireplace looked brand new. Earlier, I'd run my fingers over it, the cool smoothness bringing back memories. I remember the maids complaining about trying to clean off the soot, and rings on the mantle shelf spilt from glasses. It was never shining as white as now with its dark green stone inlays gleaming. I pointed it out to Trinity.

'Keeping that mantle spotless was one of Lizzie's jobs. When she was a skivvy it was her job to clean and light that fire every morning. Up at five o'clock she was.'

'All the staff worked hard, I think. And now it looks like they have only Carla.'

They were holding the séance at the small octagonal mahogany table in the centre of the room.

'Isn't it wonderful, Albie, how they've found all this furniture. That is the exact table where Daniel and I sat to play whist with friends.' She caressed the carved edge as she enjoyed thoughts of her fiancé. 'What fun we used to have. If it were only the two of us, sometimes we would play écarte; do you know it? It's a bit like whist.'

'No miss, below stairs we used to have a good laugh playing old maid; we could all join in, you see. Not often, mind. Not too much time down there for relaxation; only when the house was away. Our Christmas was a good time for games, whilst the upstairs were relaxing or sleeping after your dinners. Charades was my favourite but the maids all seemed to like Forfeits or Pass the Slipper.'

'Do you remember our first Christmas with the soldiers, Albie? Such fun.'

'When we dressed up? They loved it, didn't they?' I smiled at the memory. 'Look, hanging above the fireplace, they've even found Mr Daniel's ceremonial sword.'

I pointed at the slightly-curved weapon in its silver scabbard, a gold-and-silver tassel hanging from the hilt. It looked very grand mounted on its polished wood panel above an engraved silver plaque.

'Presented for services to the city by the mayor of . . . . Hmn, I can't recall which city it was. I'll go and look.'

'No! Please don't, Albie. I'd rather forget that particular item. Daniel was armed with it when . . . , on that night.'

The tears rolled down her cheeks. I'd forgotten for a moment that it was in here, the drawing room, everything went wrong. I put my arm around her shoulder as we both remembered that fateful evening. We knew our loved ones had been trapped in here with those bad men before they were taken from us.

Well now, that was easy enough, getting back in. Window still broke where the bloody bobbies caught us. Tobes got himself nabbed. Damned fool! Too bloody slow, he was. Shoulda done what I done an' shoved 'em out the way. He'll get off. Got no proof 'ave they. All went up in smoke, didn't it! Ha, ha! That Washbury; he was a waste of time. Wouldn't hurt a fly. Reckon somebody set us up with that one. And when I gets me hands on 'im, he'll wish he hadn't.

Right. Coppers all tucked up at 'ome. All's quiet. Servants in bed. Let's have a look. Where'd Washbury put that piece of paper the girl had? What with Toby messin' about with that servant, I lost sight of it. Here's a candle. Let's see the room.

Where was everyone standing? Servant 'ere. Tobes in the middle. Washbury there; by the fire. That's right, he was wavin' that bloody sword about. Fool! Doubt he'd know which end to bloody use even if he had to. I'll start over there.
***

Hell and damnation! Nothing! Bloody nothing! Not even under the furniture. So, two ways to go. He chucked it on the fire, which'd be good. Or he's got the damn thing in his pocket. Not good! Decidedly bad, in fact! A curse on that servant!

I best not 'ang around London. I'll be better off 'eading north. Plenty unrest there what with mine strikes and the like. Maybe them Yorkies could do with a bit of help against the pit owners. That'll do me.

I patted Trinity's back as comfort, trying to think of something to distract her.

'Right, here's a test for you. Without looking, there's a painting to the right of the fireplace; what's it a picture of?'

'Oh, Albie, is it the Lulworth Cove one? That was my favourite. Daniel said he'd take me there one day.' I released her so she could turn to look. 'How lovely to see it again.'

'Now, see the chandelier? How many pieces of crystal would you say?'

'I don't know . . . , a hundred maybe.'

We both gazed up at the rainbow glitters reflecting on the ceiling from polished facets. The whole thing was suspended from an ornamental ceiling rose, carved with leaves and crowns, painted gold to match the room's cornice.

'Three-hundred-and-eighty. Once a year it was taken apart to be cleaned; each piece washed and dried by Lizzie and the other maids. No smears allowed otherwise Lady Margaret would be on you in a flash. And that's a small one. You take a look at the ones in the dining room and the entrance hall. All the candles had to be lit at certain times depending on the season; never extinguished till Sir George and her ladyship were in bed. Can you imagine how long that would take? And you daren't spill a drop of wax on the carpet or furniture.'

'You're teasing me, aren't you. Oh, I can see from your expression that you're not. You mean they really did have to clean every little piece? I don't remember seeing anyone doing that either here or at my parents' home.'

'Of course you didn't. That sort of thing was done early in the morning when you were still in your bed or at times the family was away.'

'I didn't realise, Albie. It's really clever now, isn't it, this new system where someone presses a button on the wall and all the lights come on. The Americans had it too. Electric-city they call it, don't they?'

'Something like that. Did you see them using it when the carpets arrived? Someone had this magic brush on the end of a cord coming out of the wall. Clean in no time, it was.' I studied the entwined red and grey swirls and flowers on the floor for a moment. 'This isn't the Persian one that was here but it looks just like it. I don't think the old one would have lasted, 'specially after those soldiers had been tramping all over it.'

'I didn't see them brushing the carpet but I was fascinated when they did something similar on the curtains.'

We looked over at the velvet drapes framed at the window by matching gold-fringe-trimmed swags. Lady Margaret used to say they were the deep red of the summer roses near the front door. Sir George insisted it was the colour of his best burgundy.

'S'pose that's why they don't need so many staff.'

'*As* many staff,' I heard Trinity mutter before she said, 'They've even laid out the chess board on the window table. Remember how I taught you in the early years, Albie?'

'We had fun with that until it disappeared with the Americans. And you showed me a few airs on the harpsichord over in the corner. I've checked it and it's the exact one that was here. I remember one of the legs cracked and had to be repaired; you can still see the join. It was old when Lady Margaret had it so it must be well over two hundred years old now.

'She bought one of those new-fangled pianofortes when she moved to Cheshire. She befriended this family whose daughter played one they had bought for her sixteenth birthday. Lady M used to visit their home; the girl played for hours every day. Her ladyship came to enjoy the sound; the depth, she said. The girl visited often, playing airs on the harpsichord at Mulberry Hall until one day she told Lady Margaret she could "no longer call because I derive no enjoyment from the instrument." Her exact words. I was serving tea at the time and hurriedly placed her cup in her hand. Her blanched face told me she needed immediate sustenance.'

'What a spoilt little madam!'

'She was. Four weeks later a new pianoforte was delivered from Leeds along with a man from Manchester who stayed two whole days to put it into tune. The old instrument was taken away.'

'I much prefer a harpsichord. Wasn't it funny yesterday when I played a few notes. That Dr Kingsley nearly flew out of his skin.'

4

Trinity and I had heard all about the new arrivals from Carla before they arrived. Not directly, of course, but by listening in to her conversations with others.

One day she was having a cup of tea with a group of workmen and seamstresses, so we sat with the group and listened.

'He ain't no slacker is he,' said one of the workmen, 'if he owns all this.' He waved a large mug in a semi-circle.

'Please be careful not spilling,' Carla warned him.

Trinity tutted. 'Double negative! "Ain't no" would mean he is a slacker – which I doubt.' she told him. He ignored her, of course.

Mr Lovatt was worth billions Carla replied. Neither of us knew what billions were.

'Sounds like bullion,' I said, 'so it's probably to do with money. Maybe the currency has changed. Remember those American soldiers talked about dimes and dollies as their money. P'raps England has bullions and billions nowadays instead of sovereigns, pounds, shillings and pence.'

'If it's got bi at the beginning it means two or double something, you know like bi-annual or bi-monthly.'

'Right. So maybe he's worth two thousand.'

'A month.'

'A month? Pounds? Two thousand?'

'Why are you speaking backwards, Albie? Daniel had an income much greater than that.'

I counted down my fingers. 'Why, in a year that's more than twenty thousand! How many footmen is that at twenty-five pounds a year?'

'Far too many! Scoundrels, every one of them. Hee, hee!'

'Apparently his money came from a woman called Dot Com-Fenchers the nice lady just said while you were laughing at my expense. We had a skivvy once called Dot; came from Dorothy or Dora or I don't know what. Something to do with nets and webs, she said.'

'Like hairnets, do you think? You could make a lot of money selling those. Very popular, especially with older ladies, aren't they?'

'How would I know, Trinity?' I did my best sarcastic note. 'I was a scoundrel of a footman not a lady's maid. Fishing nets perhaps?'

'Go and google,' Carla said as they finished their tea. She collected the cups and left.

The sewing ladies went back to hemming the drapes; the repair man resumed his floor banging.

'I say Albie; that must be new vernacular for going about one's business. Remember those American soldiers used to say: take a hike.' Trinity playfully flapped her hand at me. 'Off you google now, Albert.'

Another time, Carla was talking about Miss Heyhough to some ladies who'd come to unpack boxes of ornaments. They all sat down amongst the piles of paper for a rest. One unwrapped a sandwich. The others wanted to know what it was. She told them it was choonamayo. Trinity and I looked at one another and shrugged.

'She nice girl, very pretty, I think so. Was engaged before but it fell off.'

'Broke off,' Trinity corrected her.

'Broke off,' one of the ladies corrected her.

'Arathea is pretty but I think skinny. With long legs.'

'Although past tense would be better as in: *was* broken off.' continued Trinity. She was ignored.

'Yes, thank you, broke off is better,' said Carla to the lady she could hear. 'She was in love but the young man had no money so . . . .'

'That shouldn't come into it,' said one of the women. 'You should marry for love.'

'Lizzie and I love each other which is why we wanted to get married. She knew I didn't have money but she believed in me. I told her, 'One day I'm going to be a butler like Shadwick, only better. He earns fifty pounds a year.' You wanted to marry Daniel Washbury for love, didn't you Trinity?'

'Course I did, Albie. I feel so lucky we found each other. He's kind, gentle and, you must agree, the handsomest man you could ever find. I love him so much. You know, the money as Daniel's wife would have been nice especially as I would have been able to help my father pay the debts on his estate. But love's more important.'

Trinity didn't know I'd once eavesdropped on a conversation between her and her father from outside the sitting room door. He'd come to stay for one night whilst Mr Daniel was away on his business. I heard raised voices from the hall and went to close the door lest anyone else should overhear. For some reason I was a little slow in pulling it to.

'Trinity, I have just read in The Times of Mr Dickens' death from apoplexy at only fifty-eight. My dear girl, I have more years than that and could be taken from you and your mother at any moment. If you do not ask your fiancé for money I, and your mother, will die destitute! Like one of Charles Dickens' characters, fit only for the poorhouse. Is that what you want? Hmn?'

'No father, of course not but I cannot plead with Daniel for money. We aren't yet married; what will he think of me?' A teacup banged onto a saucer. 'It is damnably unfair of you to ask that of me.'

'You mind your language young lady, d'you hear. The family name is at stake. I-Need-His-Money. Beg if you must but just you get five thousand out of him! A long-term loan, we could call it. God damn it Trinity, there's an article here in The Times – the man is worth a fortune. Several fortunes!'

'No father. If *you* need to borrow from Daniel then *you* must ask him. Don't use me! He will be home for lunch. If you have a good business proposition I'm sure he will try to help you.'

I heard a newspaper being slammed onto the table. Cups and saucers rattled.

'Women! God give me strength!'

I sensed it was time to move, so quickly ducked behind the servants' door. Heavy, angry, feet stamped furiously across the hall.

'Next time you can lower yourself to come back, you'll be the one explaining to your mother why she's living in a house without furniture and sleeping on bare floorboards!'

The front door slammed. Trinity's sobs accompanied her running footsteps on the stairs.

I checked the sitting room, straightened the chairs, removed the tray of china and newspaper before hopping downstairs for a quick cup of tea. Mrs Carter obliged and I perused The Times for the articles on Charles Dickens and Daniel Washbury. I knew the author's name but had never read any of his works. Anyway, I was more interested in the master so read the feature about him.

Rail Magnate Mr Washbury Receives Sword of Honour

The Mayor of the City of Oldchester has presented Mr Daniel Washbury with a ceremonial Sword of Honour on behalf of the citizens in gratitude for his services in bringing the railway to the northern city. At a banquet held in his honour Mr Washbury told the assembled dignitaries he was "delighted to unite the people of Oldchester-on-Burne with the remainder of the population of northern England at last." He thanked them for their patience while the necessary engineering work was conducted "which has resulted in the most modern terminus north of Birmingham." This remark resulted in cries of "Hurrah" and the celebratory tossing of hats, an event which was repeated when Mr Washbury attended the railway station to cut the ribbon with his sword.

Mr Daniel Washbury, the young engineer and entrepreneur is, it might be said, riding the crest of a wave at the current time. The output of his engineering works together with his ability to obtain new licences at the speed of one of his trains is carrying him rapidly on his way to becoming one of the wealthiest industrialists in the country. His stance against nationalisation of the railways has won him few friends in Westminster but his honesty in business dealings has made him popular in the burgeoning transport industry.

Mr Washbury, recently betrothed to Miss Trinity Hope of Barket House, Derbyshire, was not accompanied by his fiancée on this occasion. Her father, Mr Girling Hope, manufactures hand looms, one of the last in a vanishing industry.

'Yes, Albie, I loved Daniel greatly; as much as you loved your Lizzie. He was a good man. I . . . I-I *unscrupulous rogue, I could have feasted regularly on those offerings. But don't let me become vulgar. Especially not in the same breath as I speak of my darling Trinity.*

The first difference was her mama didn't present her to me. She was fortuitously absent. In fact, Trinity was attending a railway function in place of her mother. Her father accompanied her. He and I spoke briefly; he was in textiles, before he vanished to make business contacts elsewhere on my train. I was left to make conversation with his daughter, a pretty young lady still of teenage years. No, not pretty. Trinity was never just that. She was as exquisite and fresh and pink as the roses on the tables. She had a naughty look in her tawny-brown eyes which suggested she would do anything you challenged her to do and a puckish smile which urged you to offer her a dare. I fell in love that afternoon.

'Did I not? Oddly enough, Albie, we met on a train. As I think you know, my family home was in Derbyshire. Daniel was going to demonstrate a new train for a new railway line from Buxton Spa to Macclesfield, the silk town. He invited local public figures to join a gathering on the train journey. My father attended with me in my mother's place; she was ill. I've since wondered if he schemed it, you know.'

The woman finished her sandwich, screwed up the wrapping and dropped in amongst the packing paper strewn around the floor. Trinity watched, shook her head and tutted. We ambled away, leaving them to their work.

Trinity continued as we walked. 'Of course, I knew Daniel's name but had never seen him. Albie, he was the most handsome man I had ever seen. Tall, beautifully groomed but without a hint of fussiness popular with other men, with the deepest blue eyes like lapis lazuli which twinkled when he smiled. And, oh, that smile made my knees weak. At the end of the trip he asked if we could see one another again. When I suggested he ask my father he said, 'I don't think he is a suitable substitute. No, Miss Hope, it is you I wish to see.' How I laughed. We met clandestinely several times, shamelessly unchaperoned. I didn't care; I was in love.'

'A beautiful story.'

Carla didn't talk about the guests until they'd arrived yesterday. Rogerson Lovatt came early in the morning so he could chat with Carla about arrangements and be ready to receive visitors. There was no butler to greet them; not a footman or housemaid in sight to take their outdoor clothes or carry their trunks. In fact, they didn't have any luggage, except for a small valise each. With wheels! These they trundled across the drive, bounced up the steps and rolled across the marble floors.

Arathea was first, about an hour later than Rogerson. We rushed to the entrance hall. He greeted his fiancée at the door with an embrace as he took her bag to carry inside. The case was tiny; the same could not be said of the kiss. It was the first time we'd seen her, having heard about her

'How am I gonna explain this to the Limey inspectors?' He waved his arm in a circle to indicate the blackened, still-smoking, entrance hall, now a pile of soggy burnt timber and shattered chunks of once-beautiful moulded plaster work on an ash-covered carpet.

Captain Chadwick, his wet uniform mottled with sooty patches like a coalman's coat, nodded slowly as he looked around.

'That's a tough call, Colonel. The men did well, sir. I think it's true to say they saved the house.'

'Hmn,' mumbled the senior officer.

'The blaze on the main staircase here,' he pointed at the smoking skeleton of its corpse as the final timbers collapsed in showers of sparks, 'prevented any access. So, the guys formed a chain up the servants' stairs, along the bedroom corridor to the landing. They managed to contain the flames within the hall by pouring buckets of water from upstairs. Others threw water in the front door at the base of the fire. Apart from the hall the only other serious damage was to the wall adjoining the store; what was the drawing room, but it was safe. I've checked inside and everything's safe.'

'Any injured, Jim?'

'A few minor burns and bruises, sir.'

The Colonel nodded. 'But compared to what these guys went through before they came here, pretty small beer, I guess.

'Well done, Captain. Carry on. Oh, put a call in to HQ for me, would you. I'll be in the wards.'

Some of Lady Margaret's and Mr Washbury's gentlemen callers smoked cigarettes but those who did partake more often used a pipe. Nobody downstairs smoked except Shadwick who sometimes enjoyed a clay of an evening with a glass of claret from the cellar. But those American soldiers seemed to have a cigarette hanging from their lips every minute of every day. I didn't like the smell; burning socks. And the men were untidy. Empty packets: Chesterfield, Lucky Strike, Camel, Philip Morris; I knew all the names, simply tossed to the floor. I didn't like the way they dropped a finished 'butt', as they called it, then stepped on it to put it out. No respect.

On the day, Trinity and I could only stand watching, unable to help. I remember the awful scream of the burning oak like a wailing banshee as the stairway collapsed. Upstairs looked like it had been repainted black; covered in soot. I pictured Lizzie and the other maids having to clean it if it had happened in the old days; the footmen as well, probably; it was that important.

Once it was all over we went into the garden, sat on the grass and cried. That night and every other since then, at bedtime we had to use the servants' staircase. I used to joke with her, 'Imagine running up and down here a hundred times a morning carrying coal buckets without dropping a nugget, full chamber pots that you mustn't slosh, breakfast trays in a hurry so the eggs don't go cold and so on. Oh, mustn't forget bed warmers and hot milk of an evening.'

'I'd have been a useless servant. Night, Albie.'

I flopped down onto the bottom stair; Trinity turned and stomped through the new wall into the drawing room dragging her grumpiness behind her. Most days while the builders and carpenters were here, to escape the noise I would come to this entrance hall which had always impressed visitors in its time.

I looked around now at the rebuilt blond oak panelling, above which, still being painted, was a representation of a carved marble balustrade, a copy of the original, looking so real you might reach out to steady yourself as you climbed the stairs. The steps, almost wide enough for me to lie down fully stretched, looked exactly like the earlier ones; a dark-gold polished oak. Several large oil paintings were stacked on the half-landing awaiting hanging. I recognised them. Luckily, they were in storage during the American occupation. The blue and yellow Turkey carpet was so faded it may well have been the original one. It looked familiar.

Thinking about the Americans made me remember something which prompted a further memory. Something we discovered when they were here was that we could be seen and heard by people who'd once had that 'no-man's land' experience where the lights go out and come back on again. Where they're near to death; neither one thing nor the other.

Trinity and I used to sit by their beds listening to their stories and chatting to them. Of course, those who couldn't see us thought the soldiers were hallucinating. We had many a laugh at the doctors' and nurses' expense. One of the soldiers' favourite tricks was to have Trinity or I pull the doctors' stethoscopes off and 'float' them over the bed. The men had a special request of Trinity with the nurses. If a nurse arrived at the bedside with a roll of bandage, Trinity would grab the binding and quickly wrap it around the nurse to tie her to the patient's arm or leg.

Neither of us are the woo-woo kind of ghost. Not really. But just occasionally, for fun, we'd have a go. It was thinking of that reminded me of the night we had intruders. It was a long time after the soldiers left – twenty years or more, I suppose.

I awoke in the night to find Trinity sitting on the edge of my bed.

'Albie, Albie, wake up.'
'Wha'? Hmn? What's the matter?'
'We've got visitors.'

Back in the old days, this sort of thing could happen if there was an unexpected caller. Even in the dead of night. Many times I'd been turfed out of bed in the middle of my sleep to attend to someone: coats, drinks, slice of cold pie, whatever was needed.

One night I recall was when Sir George was involved in a particularly important case involving a royal personage. We weren't supposed to know about these things but . . . you hear things and papers get left lying around. Mind you, those things were never spoken of outside the household. It was the early hours of a summer morning; perhaps one o'clock, when I was dragged from my slumber and told to prepare a tray for an important caller. I dressed so quickly I had my breeches on back to front. I found some cheese, cold cuts and pie, poured a glass of burgundy and delivered the salver to the dining room. Later I discovered the butler and valet were at the same time attempting to rouse Sir George from his well-brandied stupor.

In the dining room I found Lady M seated with four gentlemen, one of whom had his head covered. Somehow, at a time of day when only little scampering creatures are awake, and sensible nobility are asleep, she looked fully composed and presentable.

'Thank you, Albert,' she said with a smile but also, casting her eyes sideways, a look which said: *Do not react to what you see.*

What I saw was a gentleman who I had seen only once before, waving to the crowds lining the main street as he passed through our village in an open landau. The whiskers were unmistakable. I placed the tray in front of him, keeping my head bowed.

'Will there be anything further?' I asked her ladyship.

She looked at the gentleman who shook his head in response.

'Thank you. Albert, you may leave us.' Again, that warning frown.

With a slight nod of the head, I left.

The next morning the servants' hall was abuzz with gossip.

'Visitors? Trinity! In case you hadn't noticed, I'm not a footman any longer. Let someone else take their coats.'

'I didn't mean that. There are burglars downstairs.'

'Well, they're not going to burgle much from this house, are they?'

'Listen. Music. They must have a radio contraption. Stay here.'

'Don't worry, I will,' I said as I snuggled back down.

Trinity sank into the floor; her quickest way of getting downstairs. A few moments later she was back, shaking me.

'It's a party. In the hall. Young people; my age.'

'What? A hundred-years-old?'

'Don't be silly, Albert Hapless! They have alcohol, too.'

'How many glasses did you have?'

'Please take this seriously. A party could mean dancing and if they're drunk, I'm concerned they might cause damage.'

'And I s'pose you'd like to join in the dancing.'

'I couldn't, could I.'

'Why not?'

'I've got no *body* to dance with! Hehehe! No *body*! Hehe!'

'Oh, dear. Anyway, don't worry about damage, Trinity. It's impossible to cause any further damage to the hall. It was burnt to a cinder by the American Army, remember?'

'I know but . . . . I heard one of the girls say something about having a "haunted house party".'

'I've never seen any haunting around here, have you? I'm definitely not going. You know I hate ghosts.'

'Oh, come along. I'm going down,' she said as she began sinking through the floor.

'You know I can't do that; I'll take the back stairs and see you there.' As I got up I called after her. 'Don't hurt anyone! We'll simply frighten them off,' I warned.

Trinity can get carried away sometimes. 'Try wailing; see if anyone is receptive.'

'I died, you know, on the operating table. A minute, they said. You're lucky I lived else I wouldn't be your boyfriend, Peg.'

'No, Bobby, you're the lucky one being as how I let you be my boyfriend, see.'

He always comes out with that line, especially when he meets new people. Thinks they'll be impressed. Says he saw the light. Says it gives him 'powers.' He was in a car accident with his dad driving. Got head injuries and he can't move his arms properly, although his hands weren't doing too bad that night, I can tell you.

Despite the car thing, he'd borrowed his dad's car while he was at The George in the darts' final. He wouldn't be home early. A load of us had crammed in and Jinky John followed us in his sister's little car with another full back seat. Everyone had beer except a couple of the girls who had some wine, and one bloke I didn't know who rolled up with a bottle of vodka. Bobby brought his tranny so we could listen to Radio Caroline.

'Where we going, Bob?'

'My mansion, mate.'

'What's that when it's at home?'

'You know, down Mill Lane, the Hall. Named after me, ain't it.'

'Do what?'

'The Hall. It's Ruddy 'ard, just like me, eh Peg?'

Bobby broke a window and got us all in. Someone had thought to bring candles so we sat in a circle having a laugh, drinking beer and passing round the vodka for a slug each. It was a bit spooky. There'd been a fire there like, I dunno, a hundred years ago or something, so it was extra dark with bits of burnt wood hanging off the staircase, or what was left of it. The candles threw scary shapes over the black walls.

'They're like ghost shadows,' said one girl standing up to dance to make her own patterns on the walls. 'Welcome to the haunted house party! Woo-oo-oo!'

'Ghosts don't have shadows, stupid!'

Then everyone paired up and either laid down where they were or sloped off to a corner. Bobby and me got stuck into a good snog. He wanted me to get my coat off. I said no chance; it's

November! Suddenly, someone began banging the beer cans together.

'Who's making that racket?' called a voice.

'Must be ghou-ou-ou-lies,' someone else said.

Everyone laughed.

One of the girls shouted, 'Well put your goolies away or I'll chop 'em off.'

'No you won't,' replied another girl, 'they're mine!'

More guffawing.

The rattling continued. Me and Bobby sat up to see who it was. What I saw freaked me out. In the middle of the circle the cans were jumping around on their own, clattering against each other. Then I looked up. My hand shook as I pointed. Three wine bottles were circling through the air like someone was juggling. But there was no-one there – just floating bottles.

'Look!' I screeched.

'What was that?' said Bobby, sounding worried.

'The bott—'

'Not them. That noise. Listen!'

Another girl screamed. Then another.

'Wailing!' Bobby's voice shook. 'Oh my God!' he said as he got to his feet. 'Ghosts!'

He was freaking me out. The whole thing was doing my head in.

Bobby pulled me to my feet. 'We're outta here! NOW!'

Suddenly, the blackness was filled with bodies pushing, shoving, elbowing towards the window. There was a dozen or fourteen of us; we cleared that house in about ten seconds flat. Tell you, I've never seen my mates move so fast.

We never went back.

'That showed them, eh, Albie?'

As the final one threw himself out of the window, we heard motor car engines start.

'Wait! Wait! Don't leave me!' a voice screamed. It was such a high pitch it was impossible to tell if it was a boy or girl.

And then all was quiet once more in Ruddyard Park. Except for our laughter, which, of course, no-one could hear except Trinity and me.

Smiling at Trinity's comments about my kissing Arathea, I sat and thought of Lizzie; she was the only one I wanted to canoodle. And she was shorter than me so I didn't need a box.

Oh, my dearest Lizzie, will I ever see you again? Is there truly a heaven where you're waiting for me? Can we be married?

"Albert Hapless, will you take Elizabeth Blessed to be your lawful wife; to have and to hold . . . ."

Yes, yes, yes. Please. To hold you in my arms once more, Lizzie, is all I want. I must have faith.

6

Extract from Country Days of a City Writer by
Harding Long pub'd by J. Murray 1833

*By chance, my journey to Oxford was broken, as
was the wheel of my carriage, a half mile from the
village of Ruddyard. Even though it was Market
Day the proprietor of the local inn managed to
afford me some refreshment, victuals and
accommodation for the night. What a delightful
discovery for the weary traveller!*

*An entry in The Domesday Book refers to the
settlement of Rudugeard. The name is derived from
two Old English words: rudu meaning red or ruddy,
and geard meaning enclosure or area (similar to
today's yard). From this we find Ruddyard, the
modern name for the village.*
*The first part signifies the red clay soil bordering
the banks of the river on which the village's
prosperity was founded. Thus, we can easily see the
connection: Red soil enclosure; the place from
where the clay was mined.*

*It is likely the river which flows in an arc to the
south of the village was originally known by the
same name but is now simply called River Yard.*

*In the morning whilst a repair was being effected
upon my wayward wheel, I toured the village; in*

truth, little more than a hamlet. The village boasts several shops, the charming 16th century church of St Thomas the Apostle, The St George and Dragon Inn, in which I was accommodated, a flour mill, and the clay works. Numerous farms and smallholdings are to be found in the surrounding countryside, many being tenants of the estate of nearby Ruddyard Park which was under construction at that time in 1830 but is now very probably complete.

Livestock day is Thursday weekly in the Market Square adjacent the High Street. Additional days occur during the month for which visitors should consult the announcements outside the inn and in the church porch.

My visit was during the first week of July as the weather was turning warm. In a field close to the inn and opposite the church, preparations were underway for the annual fair celebrating the feast day of St Thomas the Apostle on the 3rd of the month. Helpers were in good spirits as they constructed children's rides, stalls and colourful tents.

Every person with whom I passed the time of day I found to be pleasant and helpful, none more so than the vicar who provided the historical information of the village's designation.

Sir George Kingswood commissioned the building of Ruddyard Park in 1830 as a gift for his new wife, the young Margaret Page who immediately became Lady Margaret Kingswood. He was a successful and wealthy lawyer at the Chancery Division of the High Court of Justice. This piece of history was related to me by the then first footman when I joined the household, aged ten, in 1859. Words like lawyer, chancery and justice meant nothing to me.

How would I know such words? Neither of my parents could read or write. My dad, brought up in the country, made fences on the estate; that's all he knew. My mum wove baskets and looked after me and my sister. We lived by the river; easy for us to collect reeds and rushes – 'but be careful to not fall in!'

In those days everyone, including youngsters, helped with the harvest, no matter what their normal occupation. Mum and Dad set aside their tools for a few days to join the rest of the cottagers. There was an accident. When they died, Sir George found a place for me at the big house; Lady Margaret arranged for my sister to enter the employ of one of the other large estates in the county. They were kind people.

I didn't have a proper job like footman or even pot boy, I was just me. A pair of hands and a pair of feet. Albie fetch this, Albie carry that out, Albie go and get . . . , Albie help me clean . . . . I wasn't paid. I had somewhere to sleep and food in my belly. Mrs Carter, the cook, was my best friend. On days the fair came to the green she usually gave me a couple of farthings to spend. I used to love the noise and the colour. Playing chain tag or capture the flag with boys and girls from the village always had us flat on our backs laughing with exhaustion by the end of the afternoon.

One day when I was coming up to fifteen a new girl asked if she could join in.

'I'm called Elizabeth Blessed and I'm twelve going on thirteen,' she told us. 'My family has just moved to the village. My dad's a carpenter, my mum's dead and my little brother and sister don't do nothing but whinge all day long. We lives next the river, over from the mill. Can I play with you?'

It had all come out as one long sentence. I couldn't help but smile. She had long hair tied in two plaits; black and shiny like her eyes. I fell in love. So, Elizabeth, or Lizzie as we soon began to call her, joined our gang. She was different, acting more like a boy than the other girls. She was good at tag because she could run faster than any of us. All the boys wanted to catch her so they could wrestle her to the ground. It took me a little while to catch on as to why. It wasn't till they suggested playing kiss-chase I realised we were all in love with Lizzie. She refused.

A month later Mrs Carter called me into the kitchen.

'Albie, we've a new scullery maid; like you to show 'er what's what and what's where. Alright my lad, 'ere she is, off you go. 'Er name's Lizzie Blessed.'

She'd changed. The weather was still warm; it was August, so she was wearing a thin cotton frock of pale blue with rosebuds all over and pink trimmings at the shoulders. It looked like a Sunday-best, church-going one. The sun had brought a blush to her cheeks and forehead to match the ribbons on her dress. Her black hair was scraped to the top of her head into a bun like a little hat. Lizzie looked older. I fell in love again.

We became best of friends; seeing each other when our duties allowed. Some days if we happened to be given the same time off, we would walk to the village together, talking all the way. Or we'd cut across the estate to Stanwin Fields, taking a turn along the riverbank calling in at her dad's house. Eventually she asked me to hold her hand.

If we could organise it, we would sit together in the servants' hall for meals but as a skivvy she usually had to serve the rest of us or clear up. Best of all was when his lordship and Lady Margaret had to spend a weekend in London or travel up-country visiting. We weren't needed so had plenty of time to be together.

I didn't know if she loved me. I didn't know how to ask or how to tell her my feelings, I only cared that my heart felt light and my head happy when we were together. I had no idea about what boys and girls should do but as Lizzie grew older and ever more beautiful, I began to get some notions of what the right things might be. It was more than two years before we kissed; her fifteenth birthday. Mrs Carter made a little cake as she did for all of us on such days. Everyone was allowed a sip of sherry to go with it. I was on my way to the back stairs with a tray when Lizzie and I passed in the corridor. It was empty. We turned sideways so I could pass. Our eyes met. We were very close. I leaned forward and gave her lips a peck, tasting the sweetness of the sherry.

'Happy birthday.'

'Thank you for your wishes. And for that present, Albie.'

She didn't seem at all shocked at my liberty-taking. Her cheeks, matching mine, did colour up a bit pink but that might have been the sherry. Mrs Carter always said my cheeks were like a pair of rosy apples. Still are.

I floated up the stairs, across the hall and into the drawing room like a feather on the breeze, forgetting I was still a nobody. I was collared by the first footman who was waiting for the tray.

'Oy, where do you think you're going?' he whispered as I started across the carpet.

'Eh? Oh sorry.' I thrust out my arms. 'Here's the tray.'

'And wipe that silly smile off when you're upstairs.'

I remember being back in the servants' hall at the long table but with no recollection of how I got there. Lizzie was sitting by the fire, darning socks.

After that we would brush hands when we passed on the stairs or in the corridors but the chance of another peck evaded us. It was hard to be together. Even if we were, being of a certain age, Lizzie was always under the vigilant eyes of the housekeeper. I sensed Lizzie wanted to kiss as much as I did. She proved this one day when I was in the boot room and she arrived carrying a pair of her ladyship's dress shoes. On appearing she peeked along the corridor before shutting the door quickly and quietly. She came straight over, sat on top of my polish-stained apron and pressed her lips against mine for the longest ten seconds in my life.

At the door she said, 'I love you Albert Hapless.' Half-way out she turned back, saying, 'And don't you dare do that to any other girls, alright.'

I gawped at the closed door. My heart ran up and down my chest like it was trying to escape and chase after Lizzie. I looked down at my apron, stroking the knee where Lizzie had sat. With a shaking hand I touched the lips she'd just kissed. It wasn't until later when I saw Mrs Carter I realised I'd covered my mouth and chin with black polish.

Then the following two years saw a whole series of changes to the household. The second footman ran away with a housemaid and a few silver candlesticks. I was promoted to take his place with a wage of twenty-five pounds a year; a fortune to a nineteen-year-old. Lizzie replaced the maid to become a proper housemaid. The long-serving butler died. A man who'd been first footman and butler at a Buckinghamshire estate came to take over the household: Jeremiah Shadwick. Shortly afterwards, Sir George passed away; the house and the rest of the Ruddyard Park Estate went into mourning.

Black crepe tied with white ribbon was placed on the front door and bell-knob to deter casual visitors. By invitation only was the order of the day and a steady stream of close friends called or their servants arrived with arms full of flowers.

The downstairs bells were muted lest they were heard upstairs. I had to take my turn watching the bell board so Mr Shadwick, the first footman or her ladyship's maid could be informed if they were called. All staff, including those in the kitchen and stables, wore black. Tenants were given black crepe for men to wear on their sleeves, women in their hair.

At his request, Sir George was buried in St Thomas's churchyard in the village, following the funeral service conducted by old Reverend Shilling who had served for as long as anyone could remember. The next funeral he attended was his own. A few months later, villagers were awaiting the new vicar: Fr N Brimstone.

Shadwick had the task of organising the house and co-ordinating the funeral arrangements. Although I dislike the man, he was to be congratulated on his effectiveness. Despite not even being able to settle in properly, I have to say he handled every last detail perfectly, much to the appreciation of her ladyship. After that he could do no wrong – and didn't he make the most of it; lording over everyone with his pompous efficiency.

Lady Margaret wore her widow's bonnet and face veil for three months. She came out of mourning, removing her deep veil after twelve months. Trying to cheer herself, she refurnished several main rooms, inviting new guests and old friends to inspect her refreshed home. It helped but not for long. Also, she was aging, finding such an estate difficult to manage.

It was on a return visit to one of her 'old cronies', as she referred to her elderly acquaintances, that she made a decision which would change our lives. One of her closest friends, Lady Congleworthy, toured Lady M around some of the northern families for a month of socialising. She loved it. She enjoyed the company and the county.

She decided to sell Ruddyard Park after finding a smaller property in Cheshire which would be for sale in a matter of months by a widow in similar circumstances to herself. When her agent made it known the estate was for sale a buyer came forward almost immediately: Mr Daniel Washbury, an industrialist. The plan was for her to stay with Lady Congleworthy for several months until the new house, Mulberry Hall, became vacant. Lady Margaret was very generous to the staff when she left Ruddyard Park. We all wished her well and assumed that was the last we would see or hear of her. But not so.

Unbeknown to two of us, her ladyship had agreed with the new owner, Mr Washbury, to 'borrow' two staff when she moved house. Needing help with accustoming her new northern staff to her ways, she asked me and the junior housekeeper to join her for a year.

Lizzie and I were parted. That's when Jeremiah Shadwick pounced.

In her weekly letters Lizzie told me how he would sit close to her in the servants' hall or brush against her in the corridors whispering sweet nothings as he did. I suggested she speak to Mrs Carter but she was too embarrassed. When I'd been gone six months he asked her to be his wife, saying he would ensure she became housekeeper as Mrs Shadwick. He even told her I wouldn't be returning to Ruddyard Park. She told me this in the saddest letter I have ever received. I could feel her tears and hear her sobs in every sentence. I was furious and wanted to ask Lady M for permission to return to Ruddyard Park immediately so that I could punch Shadwick on the nose for his lies. I didn't tell her that.

I wrote to Mrs Carter instead, telling her all about Lizzie and me and announcing my intention to marry her. At that stage I hadn't actually asked Lizzie or her dad for her hand as it was a long way off. I told her about Shadwick and his promises to Lizzie. My letter did the trick. When I went home Lizzie told me about a conversation she'd overheard between Mrs Carter and Shadwick as she passed his door.

'You can't talk to me like that, Mrs Carter,' said Shadwick angrily.

'Can't I Mr Shadwick? Well, I just did, didn't I!'

'But—'

'I'll not listen to your *ifs and buts*. You listen to me for a change. Why're you filling that poor girl's 'ead with your nonsense? Marriage? Huh! 'ousekeeper indeed!'

'Who told you th—?'

'Never you mind, Mr Lothario. Does Mrs Wright, our *present* 'ousekeeper know you're touting 'er position about, eh? Not bloomin' likely, she don't! Lizzie Blessed is betrothed to Albie

Hapless, so you leave 'er alone, do you hear? And what's more, you know's well as I do that young Albie will be coming back to this household come August, just like 'er ladyship promised Mr Daniel. So, let's have no more nonsense, if you don't mind. And you remember this, Jeremiah Shadwick, it might be Mr Daniel what pays for your food, but it's me what cooks it and puts it in your mouth. So, no more tomfoolery with that young girl. Man in your position, indeed. Should be ashamed of yourself!'

His nose was certainly out of joint when I did come back. Especially when he found out about the letter.

7

Once everyone had arrived Rogerson Lovatt invited them to take coffee in the sitting room, asking Carla to prepare and serve it. Poor lady, she seems to do everything. I thought it would be interesting for Trinity so went in search of her, despite her sulking about my not kissing her. Never in a hundred-and-fifty-years has it ever occurred to me. I'm sure if I tried she'd slap my face and report me to . . . nobody. I sometimes forget it's only the two of us. I dissolved into the drawing room wall, materialising next to a small inlaid walnut cabinet I'd always admired. The marquetry was made from tiny pieces of ebony and ivory, some no more than slivers. The pattern showed little figures crossing bridges with garlands of flowers everywhere. I recalled hearing someone refer to it as Chinoiserie which meant it came from China where silk is made, I think. Anyway, she wasn't there so I tried the dining room.

'This is the original you know, Albie.' Trinity was seated about half-way along one side at the enormous table amongst all those chairs in her tatty dress like an out-of-place fork at a dinner setting. 'I know because I was sitting in this seat when I accidentally thumped down a knife, denting the wood. Look, there's the mark. Do you remember?'

I floated over to her. 'How could I forget? Having ignored my warnings about your consumption you were very drunk.'

'I know and I'm sorry I was such an indisciplined mistress, Albie. It wasn't long after your return from Cheshire; you told me I hadn't improved. Most impertinent! You might not remember but that was the evening Mr Outlandish, our neighbour, came to dinner. I don't think either of us will ever forget that name, will we?'

'Not for the rest of my . . . death. Ha, ha.'

'I hadn't laughed so much for a long time.'

'Or drunk so much! You were just as bad as always. Mr Washbury asked me to fetch a maid to help you from the table but he wasn't angry. Lizzie came. We took one arm each; you could hardly support yourself. Nobody was around so, unseemly as it was, I put my hands behind your knees and carried you upstairs, your head flopping on my shoulder. Lizzie was trying not to snigger.'

'I don't think Shadwick was very pleased with me.'

'No miss. After that, below stairs, he used to refer to you as 'that hot-headed hussy.'

'That's why he used to look down his nose at me.'

'It was a long way to look. And pointy.'

'True. Not like your little podgy one! Hehe!'

When Lizzie lived in the cottage, if she stepped out of her front door and crossed the road, she was on Outlandish land. James Outlandish lived with his elderly mother, a half-mile from Ruddyard Park.

His estate: Little Rudd Manor, abutted the north-western perimeter of Daniel Washbury's property at Meadow Mill Lane.

As a maid removed the breakfast plates, Mrs Outlandish said, 'The Kingswood place has a new owner, James. Did you know?'

Her son looked up from his portfolio. 'No, Mama, do we know the family?'

'Fellow called Washbury by all accounts; something in industry, I hear. Where have all the old families gone? It's all new money these days.'

He raised his work from the table to allow the maid to clear his plate. Some government papers slipped to the floor. As James collected them, he asked, 'Not Daniel Washbury?'

'That's the name. Do you know him?'

'No, but I know of him. He's a railway magnate. One of the chaps I'm likely to cross swords with in the near future if I can get my bill read in the House.'

James Outlandish was one of a number of MPs in favour of bringing the railways under government control thus transferring the industry's wealth creation to the nation from the hands of people like Daniel Washbury.

'In that case, young man, it might be a good idea to call on him.'

Several weeks later Outlandish called and left his card. One morning in late autumn he returned home from Westminster to find his mother entertaining a guest.

'James, this is Mr Washbury, our new neighbour from Ruddyard Park.'

Washbury stood to shake hands and exchange greetings. As they did so, the men sized each other up.

Mrs Outlandish watched the potential adversaries eyeing one another. She admired the younger Washbury's lean figure. He was wearing the latest fashion waisted jacket; shorter than the full frock coat worn by her son which had the advantage of covering his growing corpulence. There was also something avant-garde about Washbury's straight-bottomed waistcoat which had her wishing to be the young girl she once was. She offered a warning.

'Now before you both begin talking railways, let me say it is too much for an old woman to bear so I beg you to do so the next time you meet.' She tugged at the silk wrap of her tea gown as if to emphasise her age. 'For now, let us simply get to know one other as neighbours. Agreed?'

The men laughed as they shook hands on the deal to placate James's mother. Instead, they chatted amicably about the village, estate management, London and the weather, finding they held similar views on many subjects.

An hour later Daniel donned his topcoat for a brisk half-mile walk home.

Business commitments on both sides prevented further meetings until the summer of the following year when Outlandish accepted an invitation to dinner at Ruddyard Park.

The men strolled the grounds together; Daniel talking about railways development and James detailing his proposal. It was a friendly discussion which ended with an amicable agreement to disagree. Having got the business out of the way, they joined Trinity for dinner. Unfortunately, she'd been getting bored waiting alone and had comforted herself with a glass or two of wine, against the advice of the footman.

Socially, James Outlandish was charming. He thought Trinity was delightful; later describing her to his mother as captivating, vivacious and the very sort of woman he'd like to find. He told them stories of MPs behaviour in the House of Commons which had Daniel and Trinity aching with laughter. Some of the tales were retold below stairs the next morning. Daniel smiled, watching Trinity flirting with James as her alcohol intake increased. He didn't mind. He was less troubled by decorum than the nobility who would normally occupy a house such as his.

Eventually, Daniel spoke discretely to Albie. 'Without embarrassing Miss Trinity, do you think you could find a maid to help her upstairs, Albert?'

'I love this room Albie; Daniel used to throw such wonderful dinner parties here. I know below stairs you all used to work so hard for us. Haven't the workmen done a beautiful job on it. And where on earth did they discover this marvellous old piece?' She knocked the wood.

'Don't you remember, it was crammed into the drawing room with other valuables so it wouldn't get damaged by the army. After that, the men in bowler hats and brown coats took it away with everything else after the Americans had gone.

'Do you recall that poem we used to read together when we had our books? Wordsworth was it?'

'Longfellow. Haunted Houses. Our favourite verse was . . .

There are more guests at table than the hosts

invited; the illuminated hall
is thronged with quiet, inoffensive ghosts,'

I joined her for the last line.
'as silent as the pictures on the wall.'

Sliding my fingers over the polished wood, I walked the length of the huge mahogany table specially commissioned by the Kingswoods to seat twenty, although once we did manage a further six with a bit of a squeeze. Lo and behold the additional chairs were exactly where they used to be; two either side of the grey-and-white marble fireplace and one at each end of the room. Even the gold-coloured patterned silk wallpaper looked identical.

'It must have taken much investigation to find all these paintings, Albie. I used to find most of them rather tedious, all those boring faces of famous politicians but I do like the landscape above the mantle. Hampstead Heath near London, I think it is.'

'And the ceiling? We servants used to think it rather naughty with them semi-naked men and women and nymphs cavorting in the clouds.'

Trinity corrected me. 'The third-person *them* is redundant in your sentence. If you must use something as a demonstrative adjective, say: t*hose*, um, men and women.' I smiled at how she avoided referring to semi-naked figures. 'Thank goodness this was stored away in the drawing room which was out of bounds to the soldiers when we were a hospital. Heaven knows what they might have done to this top with their cigarettes and tin cups.'

'We did find some other spirits in there one night though, didn't we?'

'The ones who were playing cards for pretend money; their dollies and dimes. Yes, I remember. They taught us a new game. What was it? Sounded like a dance. Mazurka? Fox-trot?'

'Polka! That was it! They taught us how to play Polka. They lent us some money and we lost it all. Ha, ha! Such good fun.'

'Who was the one who couldn't stop telling jokes?'

'Can't recall his name. My favourite was about a couple of ghosts playing cards on a windy night, do you remember it? Another ghost opened the door to join the game and a strong wind blew away all the cards. One of the players scolded the ghost who entered:

"For goodness sake, why don't you come in through the keyhole like everyone else?"'

Trinity laughed. 'And the one who came in said, "Wasn't me, must have been another gust!" Hehehe!'

'We had some good times with the army. Do you remember they called themselves the Holy Ghosts because they'd been shot and were full of bullet holes.'

'Did I ever tell you how I got my name?' I shook my head. 'My mother was quite religious but my father wasn't. He was, however, a bit of a joker. I was their third child behind my two brothers. Seemingly, mummy was always talking about being 'blessed' with her children and how a third one was a holy gift. So, my dad said if they had three holy children, it was like the Trinity so the third one must be called that. And here I am: Holy Trinity.'

'And like the soldiers you've got the bullet hole to prove it. Is that what the kids called you at school? Or was it something like Trinnie?'

'Sometimes that but they liked the other end of my name – Nitty.' I stifled a snigger. 'Stop laughing, Albert Hapless. I suppose you were named after Her Majesty's prince.'

'Yes, and I'm proud of it. Mind you, when this happened,' I patted the hole in my waistcoat, 'that building Her Majesty dedicated to him was just about finished so I thought about changing my name.'

'To what?'

'Albert Hole, of course! Ha, ha, ha!'

'Very droll, Albie.'

'Anyway, I came looking for you because the new arrivals are meeting in the sitting room, so I thought we'd go and listen in. Come on.'

8

As we floated through the new door into the sitting room Carla was pouring coffee. Her head jerked up as we entered. She spilled some into the saucer; from under her black fringe her eyes searched the room.

Trinity whispered, 'She senses we're here. That's interesting.'

Carla seated herself in one of the chintz wing-back chairs. Rogerson and Arathea were on the small padded settle; the others on the more comfortable matching floral settee. I don't know how they did it but I would swear the fabric design used for the furniture and curtains was identical to the original.

I hadn't had a chance to look at the contents of the bookcase when the ladies were unpacking them; now I took a peek through the glass-fronted door at the titles. There were several by Miss Austen, a couple of Walter Scott's whose adventures I enjoyed, a Shakespeare collection; my favourites, some Wordsworth and Coleridge, and . . .

'Look Trinity, what a coincidence. Longfellow.'

I glanced over more poetry collections and a few titles on philosophy by Mr Hegel which I recognised as ones I'd tried to read but had difficulty understanding. Even Trinity struggled with those. I was about to open the cabinet then

Trinity stopped me. I decided to investigate more thoroughly later, perhaps re-read a Shakespeare play or two.

Dr Nutball had started speaking so Trinity and I sat on the carver chairs in the window out of the way. Not that we'd ever be *in the way* if no-one knew we were there.

'You know Plantagenet, the man who wrote all those books about travelling around the British Empire back in the 1800s?'

'I don't think he wrote them all, did he Kingsley?'

'Not unless he lived to over a hundred. Don't be pedantic, Rogerson. After they, the Plantagenet writers, had finished with the Empire they turned their attention to Great Britain and its family homes by which they meant piles like this,' he waved his arms to emphasise the point, 'not three-bed suburban semis in Streatham.'

'What's wrong with Streatham?' asked Zinnia.

'Its common.'

'I've been there and I didn't think it was a bad little town.'

'No, no, no, not vulgar. The common is what's wrong with the place: Streatham Common. It's messy and uncared for; it used to be quite attractive. A little green oasis in South London.'

'A simple misunderstanding in speech where the contracted *it is* sounds exactly like the possessive form of the pronoun *it*,' Trinity explained to thin air. 'Restructuring the—'

'Shush, Trinity.' Her need to correct everyone's grammar can be infuriating.

Arathea laughed, thinking the doctor had made a joke. Rogerson patted her hand.

'Is that what you have there, Kingsley?' Zinnia nodded at the old book he was clutching.

'Indeed it is.' He held aloft a rubbed-edged volume with a faded burgundy cover over yellowed pages, many of which looked ready to leave the safety of their binding. Carefully, as if unswaddling a baby, he opened to a page marked with a slip of paper. 'And here we are: Ruddyard House and Park. There's even a little illustration.'

Zinnia leaned towards him for a look. I got up so I could peer over his shoulder.

'It's very good,' I told Trinity.

'Read it to us Kingsley,' Zinnia pleaded.

'This was written in 1900. Plantagenet's reviewers had a tendency to waffle . . .'

'He should feel at home with it then,' Arathea whispered to Rogerson who grinned in response.

'. . . so I'll paraphrase here and there.

'"I approached the house via the pleasantly curved main drive from Meadow Mill Lane, the minor road leading south-west from the village. A small two-bay lodge, probably late eighteenth-century, of brick with ashlar details marks the entrance to the estate. The drive swings to approach the Hall along the centre of an avenue of trees.

'"My first sight of Ruddyard Park was of a rather grand house of the mid-nineteenth century. Built of Bath stone ashlar, the south-west front has two stories and numerous bays. The three central bays project slightly and those at either end are raised an additional story to form two towers with pyramidal roofs." He waxes lyrical here about the fairy-tale qualities and so on.' He waved his head side-to-side as he recited, '"Between the towers runs an ornamental stone balustrade, which is interrupted by a large central pediment. The entrance door and two of the ground-floor windows are also pedimented. The south-east front is of similar design but without the pedimented centrepiece.

'"The Hall was rebuilt in the 1830s on the site of the former late-medieval house; Stanwin Hall, which gave its name to the Battle of Stanwin of 1645 where the Royalist Army were trounced on their way to Oxford. The Hall built in 1500 had replaced an earlier building; a pond immediately west of the Hall may be a section of the moat round the medieval house.

'"A visitor to Ruddyard Park in 1826 wrote that he observed an appearance of neglect, "if not abandonment", although the land he thought to be good.' Kingsley edged his glasses upwards. 'Nineteenth-century particulars of this time which the writer has studied show that this state of affairs applied not only to the park, but existed on many of the farms also." Listen to this Rogerson; he talks about money. "At Mill Farm, for example, in 1826 it was considered that drainage would have to be undertaken before the farm could be let. The estate was described as chiefly fairly good pasture: houses were mostly old, and cottages and buildings had been so neglected that a large expenditure was required to make them tenantable. The gross rental of the whole estate was estimated at about £5,000. The rental value of the old house, land in hand, some fifty acres, and sporting rights over the entire estate was estimated at some £700 only, because of the dilapidated condition of the house. In 1830 something over 1,000 acres of the estate, including some of the outlying farms, were sold by a new owner. Ten years later another 1,800 acres were put up for sale."

'So, almost three-thousand acres and a house brought an income of just under six grand a year?' said Arathea, sounding shocked. She ran her long fingers through her short, dark blonde hair. 'Wow!'

I turned to Trinity. 'Almost six thousand pounds is a fortune. I suppose Sir George used the money to build the new house.'

I watched as Rogerson took from his pocket one of the tiny boxes they all seemed to carry and tapped it with his fingers. 'Something like half-a-mil today.'

'What does he mean?' Trinity asked.

'Not sure. Maybe that much money would buy you a share in a mill? You know, flour mill like the one in the village, or something?'

'Most probably a cotton mill such as those in Manchester. I read the other day . . . , well, not exactly the other day but you know what I mean, . . . people in the north of England call Manchester Cottonopolis. You must have heard that when you were in Cheshire. Daniel made lots of money because of cotton, he told me, building canals to ship it to the south and large ports around the country. Oh listen, he's started again.'

'"One's research indicated that in the early nineteenth century the tenants had common of pasture in three grounds when a disagreement arose over these rights and a reassessment was made of the number of beasts every tenant could pasture. Later when the owner, Sir John Mead, farmed the demesne lands himself, fresh disputes arose and Sir John excluded his tenants altogether from the lands. The quarrel was eventually taken to Chancery by one of the farmers. It was at that time Sir George Kingswood, a wealthy Chancery lawyer, became aware of the property. He had been searching for a suitable estate for himself and his bride-to-be. A sale was agreed and he commissioned the construction of the Hall I was then observing. It has remained largely unchanged since its completion in the 1830s."'

'Sir George made those cottages really nice. I know cos I was born in one,' I told Trinity. 'That's where I lived till my mum and dad died.'

'They were still good when we became like this. Now, of course, all but a few have fallen down.'

The doctor continued. '"Sir George passed in 1868; his widow, Lady Margaret Kingswood, sold the house to Mr Daniel Washbury an industrialist made wealthy by his investments in rail and canal building."' Trinity nudged me at the mention of her fiancé's name. '"I was aware, of course, of the notorious episode which had occurred in the house resulting in the gallows for Mr Washbury and his associates."' Aunt Zinnia gasped. 'Don't worry, my dear. Well-deserved, I'm sure. Damned traitors. The writer concludes, "My visit today was by kind courtesy of Mr Jacob Washbury, a younger brother."' Nutball removed his glasses and rubbed his eyes.

I looked around at their faces; each was spellbound by the words "notorious" and "gallows".

'That's a typical Shadwick remark, that is. I hate him!'

Trinity gazed at her hands in her lap; a teardrop fell onto her dress. I reached over covering her hands with mine to comfort her.

'I fetch more coffee,' said Carla, getting to her feet. 'You need water?' she asked Zinnia.

'I'll come with you,' she replied as the housekeeper loaded the tray.

'Good thinking, Carla. Thank you,' said the host.

While Carla and Zinnia were out of the room Arathea asked Rogerson, 'Did you know the house had a tarnished past?' He nodded. 'And you didn't tell us!' She smacked his hand playfully. 'What happened Kingsley?'

'Ah, well, the story is really interesting but let's wait for the others.'

I asked Trinity if she wanted to go so we wouldn't hear it. She said it might be interesting to hear what history said about us. I wasn't sure about that. We sat staring out of the window at the scrubland that had once been a forecourt with beautiful gardens.

Where there had once been walls, gates and corner gazebos there was now overgrown rubble and waist-high weeds. Beds around the edge of the courtyard and a statue in the centre of a sunken, parterre garden had kept her ladyship's gardeners busy. Beyond had once been well-tended parkland for walking and riding. Even further away had been the farms the doctor spoke about.

In the last hundred-and-fifty years the pair of us had explored inch-by-inch, trying every fence, wall, hedge and boundary to see if we could discover a way through to the world beyond. But no; we were tied here by the priest's pronouncement. As soon as we reached the perimeter of the estate we were held back by invisible ropes. Only if we could be proven innocent could we leave and see our loved ones in heaven.

9

'Isn't that interesting, Albie? The Battle of Stanwin. We didn't know that.'

'No, I doubt those poor soldiers did either. We did our best for them, though.'

My mind returned to the day we made our gruesome discovery. In Mr Jacob's days Ruddyard Park was not a happy household. The family were unhappy, the staff even more miserable. Trinity and I spent as little time as possible indoors, preferring to go on long walks around the estate; the countryside was beautiful. One fine spring day we were counting the new meadow flowers showing their faces in a recently ploughed field. It was one which had been sold off to pay some debts. The new owner seemed to be doing his best to return it to a useful packet of land.

'What do you think of the fencing he's put up?'

'Well . . . it's a fence, Albie. Made of pieces of wood. That's what I think.'

I tutted. 'My dad made fences for Sir George and Lady Margaret so I know a bit about them and I can tell you, Trinity, that's a fine piece of work. And that gate you're swinging on is beautifully made.'

'Wheee! You can tell it's new; it doesn't squeak.' Her wavy hair covered her face as she swung back. 'Wheee!'

'For goodness' sake, you are nineteen, too old for childish games.'

'I'm nineteen.'

'I just said that. Why has your voice gone all deep?'

'What do you mean?' Trinity asked in her normal light voice.

'You said "I'm nineteen" sounding like a man.'

'No I didn't, you did.'

'No he didn't, I did.'

'Your lips never moved. That's clever.'

'That's because I didn't speak, Albie. Huh! And you said *I* was being childish!'

'You didn't speak, and she didn't speak, I did. Down here. In the furrow.'

We looked in the direction of the words. There was a head; a ghostly one, looking up at us. The hair was brownish, like mine except he had a lot less. The face smiled showing three front teeth and lots of empty gum. I jumped at the sight of a phantom phizzog. It didn't look too good for only nineteen.

'Er, hello,' I said, unsure of what to say to a ghost. Trinity was the only one I'd ever met.

'Lovely morning, ennit. I'm Alan, come from Leicestershire. King's Man these two years now.'

'And what year *would* it be now, Alan?' Trinity queried him.

'The year of Our Lord, 1645, ma'am.'

Trinity and I stared at each other wondering who was going to tell him. She's better at staring than a hungry cat. Outdid me.

'Alan, I'm Albie and this is Miss Trinity. We've been ghosts for nigh on thirty years and we became like this in the year 1870.'

'Pleased to make your acquaintance, miss, Albie. Oh, deary-dear. So I been dead more 'n two hundred year. I wonder if the Royalists are still fighting. Bless my soul.'

'I pray someone *has* blessed your soul, Alan,' Trinity smiled at him, 'nobody blessed ours. Royalists? 1645? Albie, we read about that. It's what we call the Civil War. Roundheads and Cavaliers? Remember?'

'I didn't think it was very civil, miss, blowin' up folk, and killing and chopping 'em up. If that was civil, I'd not like to see them in a bad mood.'

I could tell Trinity was about to explain the differences in meaning of the word so I stepped in. 'Alan, what have you been doing all that time?'

'Can't go nowhere, see. None of us.'

'None . . . ? How many of you are there?' I asked.

'Hard to tell, my friend. P'raps fifty or such out of an army of a thousand or more, s'pose. Lucky ones was taken away for prisoners by the Parliamentarians. We're all bits and pieces, see. That's why we can't go nowhere.'

'Double negative, Alan. If—'

'Trinity! This is not the time for lessons!'

She opened her mouth then thought better of it.

He continued, 'Even worse since we got ploughed up, an' all. Now I'm like an old soldier down the alehouse – legless 'n' 'armless. Ha, ha, ha, ha! But if you could help me find me legs then I could get up and look for me arms.'

We hadn't taken any notice of the rest of Alan apart from his head and shoulders which was all we could see. Now I looked closer I saw the remainder of his torso covered in mud. Half an arrow was sticking out of his chest through a leather tabard.

'Do you want us to, er, get that out for you?'

'No, you're alright, Albie. It's how the other lads know it's me. We've four Alans, see, so I'm known as Arrow Alan. There's One-eye, One-ear and 'Arfa, cos he's only got 'alf an 'ead. We used to call him Brainless but it wasn't kind so we changed it.'

I got Trinity to help me sit the fellow in a more upright position leaning against the fence. We knelt beside him so he didn't have to crick his neck to talk to us.

'Grateful to you, young Albie and you miss. So, what happened to you both?'

We'd never had to relate our story to anyone else so we fumbled and bumbled our way through it. Trinity did most of the talking. When she explained about needing to prove our innocence to unite with our loved ones Alan said if we could help him leave he would try to find a way to repay us.

Alan told us his story. He'd been a labourer on a farm in a Leicestershire village since he turned fourteen. When the King's army came marching through from York on its way south to Oxford, Alan joined them aged seventeen.

'Well now, we didn't make it to Oxford. We gets orders to pass it by and march on to a place called Wallingford. Had some fun down there and was on our way back up country to Oxford when the other lot took us by surprise. And 'ere we are.'

He liked the uniform and camaraderie and didn't mind a "bit of a scrap" as he called the battles. Apparently several hundred men had been slain in his last fight but the majority of the ghosts had been able to leave to make their way home for one last visit to loved ones before leaving for the big march up to the sky. Since then the remainder had been helping one another to find their missing body parts. It was only once a soldier was whole he could leave the field of combat. We readily agreed to help Alan and his pals.

He told us he'd managed to locate his legs with the aid of another soldier just before the field was tilled.

'The ploughshare moved them but they can't be far. He was going that way so best start along there,' he nodded up the field.

We edged along the furrows side-by-side for about twenty yards then back again for twenty yards the opposite side of our fallen soldier. And back once more, further and further apart. After about an hour when the sun was high in the sky, Trinity called out.

'Albie! Over to your left. Is that a foot sticking out of the hedge behind the fence?'

I hurried over. Sure enough there was a leather boot which had been tossed aside by the blade. On the end of it was a leg. I was carrying it to Alan when my fellow searcher whooped she'd found the other one.

As she joined me, I said, 'I'm not sure it's decent for a young lady to be handling a soldier's leg, miss.'

'Pah to you Albie! A fine pair of legs, Alan, if you don't mind my saying. Do you recognise them?'

'Indeed I do. Got them boots off a body a couple of skirmishes ago. Very good bit of leather those are. If you can lie 'em down below my . . . , you know, where legs oughts to be, please.'

After positioning them we helped Alan to his feet; difficult with someone without arms to hold onto. He stood still for a minute before taking his first step. His leg crossed over in front of the other and he fell flat on his face.

'Zooterkins!' shouted the face into the earth. 'Oh, sorry, miss.'

Trinity looked at me for explanation. I shrugged. On rolling him over we realised his legs were on the wrong sides. We put them the right way around and helped him up again. He was taller than either of us.

Alan laughed as he tottered forwards like a man on stilts. 'At least you didn't get them back to front. I'd never have known where I was going.'

'No,' said Trinity, 'but you'd always know where you'd been. He, he.'

For the remainder of the day we walked with Alan looking for his arms. We met One-eye Alan who had discovered one leg and one arm since his namesake had last seen him. He used a broadsword as a crutch.

'Have to change your name to Hoppy,' teased Arrow Alan.

We saw several limbs but none for our Alan. Two of the many Johns, seven apparently, greeted us with smiles when Alan explained who we were and how we'd helped him.

'Got me back on me feet, they did.'

'Will you come back and give us an 'and?' joked one John.

The other John added, 'Or a foot or leg. Ha, ha.'

'Yea, can't be in the army if you en't go no arms, eh John.'

For the rest of the day Trinity and I drifted over the muddy furrows as Alan told us about the battle. As the red sun dipped away for its travel to the other side of the world we left for the house, promising to go back to help.

8 April 1645 Account of a Skirmish in Stanwin Fields at Rudyeard.

This night came a messenger with an Expresse proclaiming a miraculous victory it pleased God to grant our souldiers over the Royals at Stanwin Rudyeard. About twelve of the clocke today we

*received certaine notice of the Royalls being within
two miles, whereupon the Commander drew out his
forces, where he saw the Enemy (being about 700
Foot and 4 or 5 Troopes of Horse) on the other side
the River Yeard; our Commander sent a party led
by Captain Steyne to face them, and keep them in
action; which the Captain performed so well &
souldierlike that he put the enemy into a retreat;
then The Commander drew up all his Horse, &
found the royallists in a close body in Stanwin field,
where they made a stand & gave fire upon our
souldiers with their brasse peece. The Commander
charged their front, Sergeant Major Fellter on the
right wing, & Capt. Steyne on the left. Our horse
pursued theirs, killed & tooke many of them, yet the
rest were so fleet that they ranne to the hedgerows
& escaped. Our glorious Commander did not
pursue. He had another sceeme and charged their
foote, & wholly routed them, killed 217 upon the
place, and tooke above 300 prisoners, tooke their
brasse peece, all their Ammunition, muskets, pikes,
and swords. Our brave souldiers lost but 3 men and
none of any note. The prisoners taken were directed
to march towards Oxford.*

'Considering what's happened to them, they're very
cheery aren't they.'

'Yes Trinity, they are. I'm happy to help if
you are. In return, when they reach Heaven they
might find some way of helping us to prove our
innocence. If only we could have found that letter.'

'One day, Albie. But you know what those
poor fellows need? A system. Wandering about the

field as they do is not the most efficient method. What an army needs is a commander.'

'You're absolutely right, Trinity. And you're just the man for the job.'

We met again in the morning in the library whilst the family were at breakfast. She was as cheerful as a Derby winner.

'I have a plan. Tell me what you think, please, Albie.'

I stood to attention. 'Yes, Colonel.'

'Don't be juvenile.' She outlined her idea.

'Trinity, that's a real brainwave. Well done. Let's go and tell the men. We need to get as many together as possible. I'll run ahead and get them on parade, Colonel.' I saluted and ran off through the window to the fields.

Arrow Alan and several others were already wandering the furrows. I ran up and explained we needed to collect the men together. He called to those nearby, telling them to get all their mates lined up in front of the new five-bar gate.

By the time Trinity arrived there were twenty men with one or more legs standing to attention like a guard of honour.

'Gentlemen, allow me to present Colonel Hope.'

'Hope is what we need mate!' someone shouted.

Everyone laughed. Trinity stepped forward and climbed three bars of the gate so she was heads above the assembly. Her back was as straight as the gatepost.

'Good morning, men. From what Captain Hapless and I observed yesterday you are not making best use of your resources. The method has been that you wander the field in an uncoordinated fashion. When you find a limb, if it is not yours, you discard it. Is that correct?'

There was a murmur of assent. The men looked at each other, 'What else can we do?'

'But five yards away could be the owner of that arm or leg. Similarly, he might have just turned up something of yours and it might be a year before you come across it. Or a *hundred* years. Time wasted.'

There was more muttering, and mumbles of, 'She's got a good point, en't she.'

'My recommendation is this: all body parts which are discovered, unless it is your own, should be collected in one place. When you find something, you should shout for Albie; Captain Hapless, or me and one of us will take the item from you. At the end of the day everyone will come to the collection point to see if they recognise something of theirs. That place is here immediately outside the gate. That way when the farmer ploughs again our work will not come to nought. Any questions?'

Most of the soldiers stared at Trinity open-mouthed, then the gabbling slowly gathered momentum. I heard snatches of conversation . . .

'That's good, ennit.'

'Why din't we think o' that?'

'Reminds me of my mum, she do. Only prettier.'

Trinity continued. 'You need to line up across the field walking the furrows. Each man should cover three lines: the one he's in and one each side.' She waved her arms to indicate. 'That way nothing should be missed. King's Men! Into battle and let's get you whole and away!'

'Hurray for Colonel Hope!' shouted Arrow Alan.

Everyone cheered, saluted their new commander and turned back to the field.

'Trinity, you were amazing. Such a wonderful plan. Congratulations. Mr Daniel is a lucky man.'

The shouting began.

'Colonel!'

'Captain! Over here!'

At the end of that first day we had four more fully legged men than we'd started with and many more with restored arms, hands and feet. On the second morning several men with both arms had carried others with no limbs to the collection point. More and more came as the days progressed. Alan's original estimate of fifty soldiers was wildly wrong. There must have been at least two hundred.

There were so many searchers we had to recruit more collectors to assist Trinity and me. We worked dawn to dusk every day throughout the summer except when the farmer came to plough.

On several of those days I employed a number of men to come with me to the house on a hunt of a different kind – looking for Lady Margaret's letter. The soldiers, all of rural upbringing, had never seen inside such a building.

We examined top, bottom, inside and out of every stick of furniture in the house. Carpets and curtains were scrutinised, portraits and pots inspected. Nothing.

We made many new friends, feeling happy but sad every time a full-bodied man left. After waving goodbye we'd stand at the gate as they marched across the field slowly rising into the sky on the invisible stairway to heaven. Sometimes they carried pals who were whole but unable to walk. Trinity was saluted and thanked by everyone who departed, promises made to spread the word about our position to everyone in Heaven. We especially asked them to ask the whereabouts of Lizzie Blessed and Daniel Washbury and tell them we missed them. By the time the farmer's sowing began in the autumn, the last group of eight waved goodbye. Six walked, two were piggybacked.

That was a hundred-and-twenty years ago. Apart from one other group of spirits who came to visit having heard of our plight, we heard nothing more of our armless army.

10

She spoke in her native tongue to her grandmother whilst making coffee.

'Cici? Grandmama? I think we have troubled shadows in this house. I do not see them but sense their presence. I know there is more than one but . . . nothing more. I do not have all your gifts but you passed some to me through your daughter. They are here; I am sure they would like to ask for our help. Please guide me Grandmama.

Carla returned from the kitchen looking distracted. Her hands trembled slightly as she lowered the tray to the table. She looked into the corners of the room then straight at us for a moment.

I asked Trinity, 'Do you think she can see us?'

'No but she knows we're here, I'm certain. Wait.'

She crossed the room straight through the table and sat on the settee arm next to Nutball without any effect on the circle of people.

Zinnia continued to chatter away; Arathea listened.

Carla spoke quietly to Rogerson.

'Anything?' I asked Trinity when she returned.

'They couldn't see me but Carla's eyes flicked around. She senses there are spirits in the room.'

'Carla just told me she thinks we might have some unexpected company in the house,' said Rogerson.

Arathea's pale face turned even whiter. 'Oh no! Not rats. You get them in these old houses. I can't stand them. We've got to leave right now, darling.'

Kingsley Nutball studied her with his psychiatrist's eyes. 'Hmn, muriphobia; fear of rodents. Interesting.' He pulled on his earlobe, concentrating. 'How long have—?' He aimed his pointy nose at Arathea like a hungry rat.

'Stop analysing, Kingsley. And stop panicking, my darling. Carla thinks we might have some resident ghosts.'

'Tosh!' said the doctor with a dismissive wave of his hand. 'Don't believe in them!'

I squeezed Trinity's hand. 'Shall we have a bit of fun?'

She gave me her serious face. 'What have you in mind, Albert?'

'Would you like to see if you can remember how to play the harpsichord?'

'This minute do you mean?'

I took her by the elbow. 'Come on. If Carla thinks we might be here, let's confirm it for her.' On the way out I poked Nutball's cup and saucer making him slop his coffee on his trousers. 'Take that, Ratty Shadwick!'

Trinity giggled all the way as she skipped through doors and walls to the drawing room. The little instrument stood on eight gilded legs in one corner of the room, its polished cabinet gleaming, showing off the heavily grained wood to best effect. It was as elegant and dainty as its notes. The two rows of black keys looked well-used, the smaller white ones now yellowed with age.

'What shall I play?'

'You choose. I know nothing of harpsichord music other than it's pretty. You tried to teach me, remember? Play something they'll hear.' I turned around. 'Luckily, the door's open.'

'Something by Herr Bach, I think,' said Trinity as she settled herself on the small gilt chair. 'Heavens, it's been a long time. I remember how lovely it was playing for Daniel and his friends after dinner.'

'We have to upset Shadwick; start playing as soon as he begins reading. I'll go and look then hurry back to tell you. Get ready.'

I rushed off to the sitting room. Shadwick or Nutball or whatever his name is was about to open his book once more. He perched his glasses on his nose.

'Do hurry please, Kingsley. We're all ears,' prompted Arathea.

He started droning once again. '"My visit today was by kind courtesy of Mr Jacob Washbury, a younger brother, who greeted me personally at the front door with a warm handshake."'

I dashed across the hall calling to Trinity as I ran, 'Start now, start now,' before I scurried back with the notes of a delightful air in my ears. I stopped half in-half out of the closed door like the woodsman on a stopped cuckoo clock. The speaker had paused, looking around.

'Is that somebody's phone?'

I didn't know what that meant but everyone else obviously did as they all said 'No.' '"My travelling cloak was removed with the assistance of a footman. I found myself standing in a magnificent—"'

The housekeeper was on her feet staring in my direction. 'It is from drawing room. It is harpsichord.' Her pointing finger shook indicating the sitting room door. Carla was so pale in her black dress, she looked funereal.

Everyone turned to face me. Other than the beautiful notes of Trinity's playing echoing into the hall, the house was silent. As if someone had commanded it the guests got to their feet, moving to the exit. I stepped away so they wouldn't walk through me. Rogerson opened it allowing the sweet music to flood the space as they trod carefully across the hall carpet towards the open doorway and the sound. I laughed. If only Trinity could see their faces. When we were alive there was a phrase everyone used: They looked like they'd seen a ghost. Well, this lot certainly did! When the gathering neared the drawing room door, I called out to the player to stop. She did. The shuffling individuals bumped into one another as they came to a sudden halt. Carla pushed her way to the front, stepping across the threshold from the hall. She went rigid, her face pensive as she closed her eyes and took a deep breath.

Trinity and I stood beside the harpsichord, fascinated by the group. They gawped at us; well, in our direction at least; we stared at them. Other than the occasional tradesman during the repair work we hadn't really had a chance to study modern mortals, not since the Americans.

But these people were quite different. Their manner of dress was strange to our nineteenth century eyes. Trinity and I had discussed it.

'The fabric of their apparel looks so soft even compared to the finest worsteds and silks of our day,' said Trinity. 'I would love to touch it. Their clothes look so clean and new. And they wear less, don't they.'

'Have you noticed their hair? So silky. And skin? It sort of, I don't know, glows. And it's smooth, too.'

'I think everyone's bigger as well. Apart from me, I knew of no girls my height and certainly none taller.'

'They look a bit frightened, don't you think?' said Trinity.

'Yes, and Miss Arathea looks ready to faint. Nice tune, by the way. What was it?' 'One of Bach's gavottes. Actually, it might have been two; I was confused. I think I joined them together. It *has* been a long time since I played.'

'Nothing here!' grouched Kingsley Nutball. 'Knew it! Imagination. Auto-suggestion as a sub-conscious response to your mention of ghosts, Rogerson. No such thing!' He turned to leave.

Trinity stood with her hands on her hips. I recognised that stance; it spelled trouble. 'Is that so?' Before I knew it Trinity pressed three keys.

Inside the instrument three strings were plucked producing the familiar doh-ray-me.

Rogerson caught his fiancée as she swayed. Aunt Zinnia gasped; she was getting a lot of practise. Carla's hand went to her mouth, covering colourless lips. The sceptical doctor slowly rotated on the spot.

'I must have my hearing tested,' he said, staring at the harpsichord. 'I keep thinking I hear music.'

'We all heard it Kingsley. Don't be such an obstinate fool,' said his host.

Zinnia laughed. 'I say, how spooky.'

'I will look at the instrument in case something is . . . .'

'What Carla? Something is what, hmn?'

'I don't know. Broken, maybe.'

'Ha, ha, ha. You'll probably find one of those old paper rolls inside so it can play itself.'

Nutball followed Carla to the harpsichord; the others shuffled behind. I pulled Trinity aside so we didn't get walked through. The thought made me shiver. I stood alongside the doctor. He looked and acted more and more like Jeremiah Shadwick. I wanted to pay him back for trying to take my Lizzie from me and for being so obnoxious. Sitting on top of the instrument's cabinet was a heavy silver candlestick. I remember it was one of my duties to ensure it was lit to illuminate the sheets of music for the player. As Nutball leaned forward to examine the interior I knocked the candlestick to the floor aiming for his foot. I missed.

'Please take some care doctor. This worth much money of Mr Lovatt,' Carla complained.

'I didn't . . . .'

I pulled Trinity away, leaving them to argue. 'I've another idea. Back to the sitting room. Quick!'

'Albie, you are using the word "quick" as an adverb in a truncation of the imperative "come quickly", therefore you should be advising "Quickly."'

I've been ignoring Miss Trinity Knowall's grammatical advice for a hundred-and-fifty-years and did so now as we hastened to the other room.

'Look!' I pointed at the coffee table. Three of the little magic boxes they all carried sat there. 'Sometimes when they tap those things they play tunes. Let's see if we can do it.'

'Such fun. This must be Arathea's; she was sitting here.'

'And this one's Shad—, Nutball's.'

We sat tapping, puzzled by the tiny pictures and symbols. Sometimes a box appeared with Yes? No? written inside. I always tapped No? just in case. I noticed Trinity was sliding her finger up or down the front which I'd seen them doing so gave it a try.

'This must be how those explorers felt translating hieroglyphs. Oh, look, I've got a list of names,' she said. 'Aunt Zinnia's at the top. Have you got that?'

'No, I've got a painting of a lady. Aargh! What's that?' I dropped the box on the carpet as Zinnia's box next to me started playing music. It stopped.

Trinity was laughing as I retrieved the thing from the floor. 'He, he, I think I did that. I patted her name on this list then a green circle and that happened. Watch.' The box vibrated on the table making its strange music then stopped. 'See.'

'How did you find the list?'

'I don't know but if I rub the front like this the names move and more take their place. Ah, I see, it's in alphabetical order. Benjamin, Bob, Brenda . . . , now I'm on Cs and Ds. It's very clever, Albie.'

Trinity turned the instrument over to try opening it with her fingernail to see inside. I tapped her on the wrist to stop her. I sat next to her and watched as the names moved.

'Stop, stop! There's Dr Kingsley N. Hit it.'

She did. Opposite us his box rattled on the top, making a different noise: a sort of bing-bong. Trinity stopped it and continued scraping the list.

'How do you make the music stop?'

'When I tapped on the name the list changed into this,' she showed me what to do, 'and I touched the red button. Red for danger, I thought.'

'Rogerson.' She tapped it.

I looked around the room. 'Nothing's happening. Where's his box?'

'I know. Remember he looked at it earlier, when he talked about buying half a cotton mill? He put it in his pocket. Let's go and see if it's humming a tune. This is great fun.'

Just as we arrived in the drawing room through the wall next to the Chinese cabinet, Rogerson was near the door staring at the shiny singing box in his hand. He turned to Arathea who was standing with the others beside the harpsichord.

'Darling, why are you phoning me?'

'I'm not. I haven't got my phone here.' She showed him empty hands.

Trinity and I sniggered.

'Did you hear that?' I said. 'She called it a phone.'

'Why do I know that word?'

'The Americans had them, remember? We thought they looked like bones; the sort you'd give a dog, only black.

'Yes, they put one end to their ear and spoke into the other end and somebody, somewhere else could hear them. Extremely clever, we thought. But those phone things were all connected with wires. These aren't.'

'Different sort, maybe.'

The others joined Rogerson having lost interest in the instrument.

'My phone's in the sitting room,' said Arathea.

'Well then, someone is in there using it because my phone says it's you. Look.'

'It is the spirits,' said Carla.

We were laughing so much we had to sit down.

'Pah!' grumped Nutball pushing through the group into the hall, heading for the other room.

Holding our sides, we followed them to the sitting room where they clustered around the coffee table to pick up their shiny black boxes – phones.

Arathea touched hers and the tune on her fiancé's stopped.

'Someone *has* been using my phone.' Her voice rose to a hysterical pitch. 'I didn't leave it like this.'

'You must have done.'

'Are you absolutely certain?'

'It couldn't have done it by itself.'

'OK everyone, let's stay calm,' Nutball's voice was soothing like a doctor's. 'Carla was kind enough to bring us some fresh coffee a few minutes ago,' he smiled at her, 'so let's settle down with our drinks and finish the history. Arathea, why don't you read it; give everyone a rest from my voice.'

'Good idea,' I said to no-one in particular.

She accepted the dilapidated book as if handling a delicate rose about to drop its petals. He indicated where to begin.

'So, the writer's just arrived to be greeted by Jacob Washbury. "I found myself standing in a magnificent hall rising from which was a splendid polished oak, broad stairway. The most notable feature of the staircase is the painting of the walls and ceiling. One's attention is instantly drawn to the paintings around the stairwell of the lives of selected Greek heroes. As glorious as they are, even those are surpassed by a monumental representation on the ceiling of Mount Olympus and its gods." Rogerson is going to reproduce that aren't you darling?'

'Yes, but using modern reproduction techniques, I'm afraid. Those originals must have taken years.'

'Next he seems to go on to detailed descriptions of every room in the house. Might be a bit too much. Shall I skip to the Daniel Washbury story?'

They all agreed. I patted Trinity's hand. She looked composed. Arathea took up the yellowed volume once more. Her lilting northern accent was easier on the ear than gruff Nutball.

'"By the standards of the day, Daniel Washbury was of a younger age than most men acquiring an estate of the proportions of Ruddyard Park. If the reader will indulge me for a few sentences of historical information.

"Upon completing his education Mr Washbury immediately entered the burgeoning railway industry as an engineer. Astute investments in rail shares and canal development rapidly made him a wealthy man although only in his middle twenties. He soon had his own engineering works and was connecting towns and cities throughout the country. It has been reported he had an interest in developing a flying machine after being commissioned by Mr Francis Wenham to build for him a steam engine to power a fan for testing such structures. He was quoted as saying he believed it had a 'commercial potential.'

"The nineteenth century saw a steady increase in the desire of government to become involved in railways. The Railway Inspectorate was established in 1840, to enquire into the causes of accidents and recommend ways of avoiding them. As early as 1844, a bill had been put before Parliament suggesting the state purchase of the railways; this was not adopted. There were calls for nationalisation throughout the 1800s." Arathea glanced at the coming paragraphs before continuing. 'Wow! This is where it seems to get really interesting. Listen up.' It came out as oop.

I waited for Trinity's usual grammatical correction. Silence.

"'One such proposal was made by a prominent politician James Outlandish, landowner of the Little Rudd estate abutting Ruddyard Park. In the late summer of 1870 Daniel Washbury together with his fiancée, the rebellious Miss Trinity Hope, hosted a gathering at Ruddyard Park of other people interested in the continuing success of rail. Their aim was to prevent the nationalisation of the rail network. The small assembly contained the notorious anti-Gladstone campaigners: Bertram Oddfellow and Toby Bristler.'"

Trinity didn't react to the description of her as rebellious. She fidgeted. I understood; I also found it difficult to sit still.

'Did Daniel really believe in flying machines?' I asked.

'Oh, yes. He said one day the sky would be full, and spoke to me at great length about them and Mr Wenham's ideas but . . . but . . . he didn't get a chance to build the engine for him before . . . that night. Oh, Albie. I miss him.' Trinity sniffled.

Together we got to our feet. Turning towards the window we gazed into the distance, lost in our thoughts. Neither of us was comfortable about the events of that evening. After all, it was the night we died

11

In our early years we had discussed it so many times, day after day trying to make sense of everything.

Apart from Trinity attending the meeting, everything Arathea read was accurate, including the names of the gentlemen involved, although we didn't discover that until several days later when Trinity, by then a ghost, overheard a conversation and related it to me. We were sitting on the pile of bricks that had once been the stable wall; the rubble that now covered our mortal remains. She looked over her shoulder as if somebody might be listening. We hadn't become accustomed to the fact no-one could hear or see us.

'Albert, it appeared that the proximity of Ruddyard Park to Mr Outlandish the MP's estate was paramount in their plan. Daniel expected them to discuss a campaign or a petition to Parliament but the two of them proposed assassination. They had gone to see Daniel under false pretences, I'm certain. My Daniel was not a killer. Mr Outlandish came to dinner once with his sister and some friends of Daniel. He was a nice man but a little serious.'

'We must tell someone, Miss Trinity;' we were still being formal with each other back then, 'we have to tell people Mr Daniel's innocent and then he can tell them we had nothing to do with it.'

Now, gentlemen, pay attention. Silence and stealth are crucial for tonight's proceedings. For your orientation, we are standing in Meadow Mill Lane. Our objective is due south. Move into the field, gentlemen, if you please, lest we draw attention from any late passers-by. The Reverend here will take us behind the carpenter's cottage over there. See, on the riverbank opposite the mill? He will lead us to an adjoining path; he tells me we would never find it on our own. Quieten down; enough laughter. Please respect the vicar's local knowledge. There he will leave us to do our job.

The track leads directly to the rear of the house via the kitchen garden. Correct Reverend? Excellent. As you see, the moon is in its third quarter, luminosity is still high, so we must keep to the tree line. There is a stable block to our left which will afford cover along with some full yew hedges. Directly ahead at the northernmost corner are the windows to the drawing room where the gathering will occur. It is not clear how many are attending. More central is the kitchen door but I am reliably informed staff will be in their beds. However, keep a sharp eye; lookouts may have been posted.

Our intention this evening, men, is to arrest these scoundrels and place them in the hands of justice. We do not know if they are armed. You may fire your weapons in one of three situations. One: to warn an adversary, two: disable him if appropriate; for instance, if attempting escape, or three: to protect yourself or others from injury. There is a possibility of explosives being secreted on the premises but we will attend to that once we have apprehended these damnable . . . excuse me, Reverend . . . wretched traitors.

You all know your positions. To the front; the door is unlocked, the side; be prepared to be summoned in either direction, and men at the rear; access will be via the windows which you will need to smash. Please check your weapons and ammunition, gentlemen. Absolute silence from now on. Follow Reverend Brimstone, if you please, and God's speed.

The first thing I knew about the whole affair was when Trinity hunted me down in the kitchen garden. It was a warm summer evening; all my duties were completed and I was sitting on a low wall breathing in the scent of the herbs. I picked a sprig of rosemary for Lizzie. I was expecting her shortly. She'd gone to deliver Lady Margaret's letter to Mr Washbury. I knew if I'd kept it Shadwick would have searched my belongings to find and destroy it. That's why I gave it to her for safekeeping knowing he wouldn't take the chance of being found in the females' quarters. No matter what excuse he came up with he'd still have his wages docked; he wouldn't risk that.

I remember I'd just tucked the sprig into my top buttonhole when I heard a scuttle in the yew hedge beyond the garden. Rats, I thought, Mrs Carter won't want them near the kitchen. There was a garden cat but it was useless. I'd caught more rats and mice for Mrs Carter than the cat ever had. I picked a few stones from the path, pitching them into the blackness. When I heard it again I clapped my hands to frighten them. All was dark and silent.

No-one knew there were visitors in the house. Not Shadwick nor any of the footmen or maids had been told to be on duty so hats'n'coats'n'cloaks hadn't been taken, no drinks were ordered or served. Even Miss Trinity didn't know. All we knew was Mr Daniel was in the drawing room because the candles hadn't been extinguished. Lizzie certainly hadn't been informed or she wouldn't have intruded on the meeting no matter how important our letter.

Anyway, there I was tossing a couple of pebbles from hand to hand, dreaming about the future Mrs Hapless when Miss Trinity in a flash of gold satin came running at me from the back door. What on earth she'd been doing in the kitchen I couldn't imagine and didn't get a chance to ask. I was too surprised finding out that someone from upstairs had been able to find their way below stairs.

'Albert, Albert! You must help me!'

I immediately began buttoning my waistcoat, undone because I hadn't expected to be called to serve. Lizzie's rosemary stem dropped out. Before I had a chance to pick it up Trinity was dragging me by the arm in the direction of the stables around the side of the house.

'What is it, miss? What's happened?'

She was out of breath. 'Daniel . . . two men . . . Mr Outlandish,' she paused and breathed deeply. 'Murder!'

'Slow down, miss. Who's murdering who?'

'Need to warn him. There are two men in the house plotting with Daniel to kill Mr Outlandish. Come quickly and help me with the small trap and a horse or pony. I must get to him.'

I couldn't fully grasp what she was saying but she was insistent on me doing something.

'But the stableman won't be—'

'Won't be there; I know. That's why I need you.' She tugged my sleeve so hard I was afraid it would rip off at the seam. 'Quickly now!'

'But there's nobody in the house. If there was I'd know it cos I'd be needed . . . to attend . . . to . . . them. Whose carriage is that? It's not one of ours.' I was staring at an ancient black hackney standing next to the stable. The horse, and that's being polite, must have been the same age as the carriage, turned a disinterested head in our direction.

'It must belong to those men. Perfect!' Her face was a white oval against her black hair and the darkness. 'I'll take it to warn Outlandish then they won't be able to do their dirty business.'

In the darkness we crept along the old stable wall in the footings trench being dug for the additional stalls. The only sound stirring the silence was of muffled feet on the stony path; that's not rats, I thought. The stillness of the night suddenly shattered.

A deep military-sounding voice bellowed, 'Put down your weapons or we will shoot!'

I saw as much fear in Trinity's eyes as she must have seen in mine.

I heard a window smash, much shouting from the house. The words "Special Police Service" were called out.

'Put down your weapons!'

'You are surrounded, don't move!'

'Don't shoot!'

'Albert, help me into that carriage so I can get away.'

I'm fairly well-built, not afraid of a fight but this was different. I grabbed her arms. 'They've got guns, miss. They might shoot. Put your hands in the air to show them we are unarmed.'

A gunshot from the drawing room side of the house made us jump. It was the crack of a pistol not the boom of shotgun. There was another; then a third. Sounds of men's voices in a scuffle were followed by heavy steps, running fast.

'Oh! Daniel!'

A cry. 'He's coming your way, sir!'

Another voice. 'He's got a gun! Watch out!'

Then many things happened at once. It was like one of those silly plays I used to see on the village green when the travelling entertainers came. Lots of people shouting, figures running everywhere, then more shots were fired and it became even more like bedlam.

A heavy-set man, coat flapping, running along the trench to the old carriage aimed his fist at Trinity's stomach knocking her into the ditch. I made a grab for him but felt a thud in the chest knocking me down as if I was a stick of a child.

'Stay where you are!' ordered the deep voice.

The man ignored the command, tugged open the hackney's door and jumped inside away from the yelling and gunshots.

I clambered out of the hole, lifting my young charge after me.

'You're bleeding! Are you alright?'

A dark stain spread across the bodice of her gown.

I pressed my hand to a sudden searing pain in my chest. I grabbed for her as she stumbled face first into the trench. My legs wouldn't let me stand. As I dropped backwards to join her there was a blast and sheet of flame as if the gates of hell had opened onto the earth. Slowly as drifting snowflakes I watched as bricks and mortar, slates and rafters seemed to float from the black sky, pounding Trinity and me. The bottom half of a hackney door landed between us. I lay still, feeling nothing.

'Albert? Are you alright? I can hear voices.'

'I think so. Let's see if we can climb out. Shout, miss, so they know we're here.'

'Help!'

'Help us, please!'

We sat upright and found ourselves perched on the remains of the old stable wall. The hackney carriage was no longer in place, nor the horse. Several men lounged where the wall had been; they were staring at the rubble. All wore dark topcoats, despite the warm evening, a couple even had shoulder capes fitted. It's a footman's job to notice these things. One was dressed for shooting: peaked hat, short jacket and gaiters. The others, one excepted, were sporting bowlers. None of them looked particularly like police officers. The one standing apart wore a top hat. He was in conversation with a priest, distinctive in his capello romano soft felt hat. He looked as though he was in the wrong play.

'Wait here,' I said to Trinity. 'I'll see what I can find out.' I approached the group, brushing myself down. 'Good evening, sirs. Albert Hapless, footman to Mr Washbury. What a to-do, eh? What's been happening up at the house then?'

One of them tapped out his pipe on a brick, preparing to address me I thought. He turned to his colleagues, ignoring me.

'While you lot was busy smashing windows we simply marched in through the front door and into the drawing room, easy as pie, didn't we Jim?'

'Sorry. Excuse me . . . .' I tried to butt in.

'Yeah, straight in. Took 'em by surprise. 'Cept that Washbury was waving a sword around like he was expecting a fight.'

'Probably tipped off by these two.' The speaker stared past me as he nodded at the pile of debris.

'Hello?' I said.

'Must've been. I heard the servant give a signal by clapping.'

'I was scaring away rats! If you knew Mrs Carter—'

The other began refilling his pipe as he spoke. 'That must've told the girl to warn them before she got away cos a minute later she comes haring out dragging him to the carriage with the bomb in it.

'Girl! That's Miss Trinity Hope, Mr Washbury's fiancée,' I corrected him. 'Bomb! What do you mean, Bomb?'

'Tell you what, that Outlandish MP fella's a lucky one. That was meant for him. I think the plan was for her to waylay him on the road on his way back from London,' he consulted his pocket watch, 'about now. You know, pretty little damsel in distress by the roadside. Get him to take a look at her carriage . . . ,' the men sniggered, 'now, now, lads . . . then take cover and Boom!, up he goes on his way to heaven.'

'You can't talk about a young lady in that way—'

'Instead up *she* goes with her personal footman to escort her to the pearly gates.'

The top-hatted gentleman was approaching accompanied by the vicar causing the others to stand upright like soldiers coming to attention. I assumed he had seniority.

'Is there any chance of life under that?'

'Nah, sir. I shot the lackey and Will here got the girl. Oddfellow was with 'em so I might-a nicked him and all.'

'Saw 'em both go down sir, just before the carriage blew up.'

'Shot! Shot? You shot me? How dare you?' I looked down at my shirt and waistcoat. A bloody hole had made a mess of my uniform. I turned to look at Trinity remembering the blood stain on the front of her dress. She wiggled her fingers in a friendly wave. I turned back to the man. 'You shot Miss Trinity? Mr Washbury will not be happy!'

'What of the bomber, Oddfellow?'

'Might be more like what's left of the bomber, sir. We haven't found him yet so either he got away or there's bits of him over there with the poor old nag. It's not pretty. Won't be able to tell till the morning.'

'If he did escape, sir, he'll have a hole in him somewhere. I'm sure I got him,' said the man in the peaked cap.

'Right-o, chaps, well done. Good show tonight. He tipped his hat brim in salute. It was the Reverend here who gave us the tip. Off you go, Father. Do the necessary; last rites and all that.'

I expected him to remove his wide brimmed hat for the blessing but he kept it on. 'Not for those two filthy traitors, sir. By their despicable deeds; abetting the criminals, they are as guilty as if for the sin they had planned to commit – a foul murder of an innocent and upright citizen. Mr Outlandish is a fine man and patron of the village church.

'Let this be their grave – this unconsecrated ground. I condemn their souls to remain bound to this estate for all eternity – until the Day of Judgement!'

'But Father, whilst we *think* these two were involved, we have no proof until we question Washbury and Bristler other than their proximity to the scene of the crime. Surely if there is doubt you should err on the side of compassion. Is that not what God—'

'Sir, in matters of religion I believe my standing is greater than your own. I would not presume to dispute the law with you, Commander, so—'

'But—'

'But, if their innocence one day be proved beyond doubt, sir, then the Lord will know and give his blessing, happy to welcome them into the Kingdom of Heaven. I bid you good evening, sir, and God bless you gentlemen for your patriotic deeds this night.'

As I returned to Miss Trinity, not knowing what to say, I overheard one of the men, 'He's a rum one and no mistake. Wouldn't like to do confession with him. Be more than a couple of Our Fathers for penance, I'd say.'

The others' laughter echoed across the garden.

I arrived with Trinity to the sound of raised voices I recognised.

Mr Daniel and another man; tall, skinny chap, were being pushed by men I assumed to be more police officers.

'Daniel! Daniel!' called Trinity as she ran to him, arms outstretched.

'Release the girl,' called Mr Daniel, 'she's done nothing. She's just a servant for God's sake.'

'I'm innocent, sirs, please unhand me. I done nothing,' my Lizzie yelled as two men dragged her along the path.

'Hold on, Lizzie, I'm coming.'

I ran to them, shouting to leave her alone. I took a swing at the first one. I felt nothing. I thought I must have missed so I got closer and threw him another punch. No effect. He didn't falter; simply

'Was she hurt? That was the man who shoved you into the ditch; the one who got away according to the police – or got blown up. Mind you, I don't see any other ghosts hanging around, do you? If I find him, I'll kill him if he's harmed my Lizzie.'

'I don't know what was under discussion but that fellow obviously believed it should be secret. He shouted at Lizzie.

'"Are you spying on us, young miss. Come in here!" he said, yanking her across the threshold. "What's this you've got in your hand? Been writing it all down have you?"

'The door remained open so I could hear every word. He snatched the paper from her. She screamed, "Give that back! It's for Mr Washbury from Lady M—"

'"Shut up and don't you be talking back to me like that, girl."

"It's her blessing for me and—"'

I turned to Trinity. 'It was our letter to tell Mr Washbury she agreed to our marriage. What happened to it Miss Trinity? Did she give it to him? If she did then we can be wed within the month. Please tell me she did.' Then I remembered my condition.

'The other man? The one the police just dragged across the path with Daniel? Skinny fellow. He was in the room and took the paper from his acquaintance.

'"Take this and hide it Washbury," he said passing it over. "And let's get back to talking about eliminating Outlandish tonight. It'll be on the road not far from your gates. We'll blow him and his fancy ideas sky-high."

'So, Mr Washbury's got the letter? If we can find it then Lizzie and me—'

She interrupted. '*I* – not *me.*'

'Hmn. Anyway, we can prove our innocence because the letter gives us both a good character. And if I'm blameless then you must be cos you wouldn't associate yourself with a conniving servant, would you? They'd see that.' I was wringing my hands. 'What is that thing they say about guilty people knowing other guilty people?'

'Do you mean the expression: Guilty by association?'

'That's it. So, you'd be innocent by association. What did Mr Washbury do with the letter?'

'I don't know. The next thing I saw was Daniel brandishing that sword from above the mantle. He was shouting but I couldn't hear him above Lizzie's screams as she fought to get away from her captors.

'Albert, I wanted to go in and help her, I really did but . . . I realised I had to warn Mr Outlandish. They were going to kill him.' She took my hands in hers to comfort me. 'I was certain they wouldn't kill your Lizzie.'

'I understand, Miss Trinity. You acted for the best. We know now you were right; they didn't harm her.'

'That was when I rushed to find you. Albert will help me, I told myself. And look what happened. I got you killed.'

'And yourself. Now, who's this coming?'

'Look Albert, all the staff have come out. What's going on?'

Mr Shadwick and Mrs Carter led the way; housekeeper, footman, maids all following. They came from the side of the house on the same path we had used coming from the stables.

'I always said she was a firebrand, that Trinity Hope. Mark my words, I said, she'll be trouble for the master,' crowed Shadwick.

Trinity got to her feet ready for a fight. I put a restraining hand on her arm as she started to walk towards him.

'It's no good miss, he can't see or hear you.'

She strutted over to the group, went right up to Shadwick saying, 'Such impertinence! How dare you!' and slapped his face – or tried to. As with my swing at the policeman, her hand passed straight through him. She looked back at me then tried again. Same result. Luckily, this was before we realised we could touch objects but not people. Otherwise she might have picked up a flowerpot and smashed it on his head. Trinity turned to me as if for advice. I shrugged.

Then she saw the funny side of it. She gave me one of her little giggles, spread her arms wide as if to embrace the party and walked right across them.

'Come along Albert, you give it a try. Such fun!' she called as she stepped into their centre and out the other side. 'Makes one feel a bit giddy. Wheeee!'

She took my hand and guided me through with a shiver. The sensation made me think of when we were kids playing in the river in summertime. You could be standing in the middle enjoying the warm water when suddenly a cold current would come from nowhere and pass over you. Two seconds later it was gone.

'I can't believe it,' said Mrs Carter, tightening her shawl. 'That poor young girl; shot, dead and buried all in one night so that policeman said. And the vicar refusing to bless their souls. That's a terrible to do. And what of poor Lizzie? What was she doing up there in the drawing room? She weren't on duty. Dragged away in manacles, poor mite.'

Shadwick nodded in agreement. 'Yes indeed. But it's obvious to all who meet her she's innocent; Lizzie'll be home soon. As for young Hapless . . . .'

One of the skivvies piped up, 'Beggin' your pardon, Mr Shadwick but why'd they shoot our Albie? 'e was allus nice to folk 'e was.'

'You're right my girl,' said Mrs Carter, throwing one of her accusing looks at the butler. 'Make a nice couple, 'im and Lizzie.'

'Not now, they won't.' Shadwick grinned like a wolf. 'Got what he deserved according to the police officer; him and that hot-headed girl. They were in it together. Traitors to Her Majesty The Queen, the pair of them.'

My blood boiled at that remark. Now it was my turn to take a swing at him but like Trinity, I missed. She watched, hands on hips quaking with laughter.

'Getting a bit chilly out here,' said Mrs Carter, moving away from Shadwick. 'Let's go in and I'll make us some cocoa.'

Trinity and I watched the gathering turn towards the rear of the house. How I wanted to join them; I love Mrs Carter's cocoa. As we sat once more, I imagined I was cradling a cup in my hands sitting in the servant's hall.

'Albert? Who were all those men in the garden?'

'When it all started I heard one of them shout: Special Police Service.'

'They didn't look like policemen, Albert.'

'When I was up at the Cheshire house the new butler Lady Margaret employed used to read the newspaper to the staff "for your heducation and hedification" he used to say. That's how he talked – used to call me Halbert.'

'That little girl, the scullery maid, called you Albie. Is that how you're known to your friends?'

'Always have been, miss.'

'Hmn, I see.'

'Anyway, I can recall him, the butler, telling us the Queen had agreed to the "formation of a different type of police force to investigate troublemakers plotting against the interests of the country." I think those were the words. He told us about Mr Bismarck's spies and the Frenchies who live in England but who work for Napoleon. Even some who want to murder Queen Victoria herself and overthrow the government. Can you imagine?'

'Shocking. I suppose that's why they all carry firearms.'

The next morning I was downstairs as usual; I didn't know what else to do. I overheard Shadwick ask the housekeeper in his officious voice to conduct a thorough search of Lizzie's belongings whilst he and the first footman rummaged my things "for any evidence that might be of use to the officers of the law." I might have known he'd find a way of getting into the female quarters. I knew what he was after but if Miss Trinity was right in her observations the piece of paper Shadwick wanted was somewhere in the drawing room. I realised if no-one could see me, I could go wherever I wanted so went on my own treasure hunt.

The door was open when I arrived so I simply walked in, bold as brass. I scoured every inch of the room, even lifting the edges of the carpet. I was going through one of the cabinets when one of the girls came in and began wiping the furniture top surfaces. I was about to hide when I realised it no longer mattered. I called out her name. No reaction. When she reached the fireplace, she moved a vase aside, recovered Mr Daniel's ceremonial sword from the mantlepiece, replaced it in the scabbard which was lying on a chair seat, and hung it in place. After standing back to check it was straight, she left. Mr Daniel wasn't a violent or aggressive man; I was puzzled by Trinity having said he was "brandishing that sword". It didn't seem like him.

Without thinking I approached the fireplace and removed the weapon from the wall. Drawing it from the sheath I waved it around at an imaginary opponent. But he had a real name: Shadwick. I thrust at him. I parried his attacks. I sliced at his torso. I ducked his blade. I lunged and feinted. I slashed and swung. It was as if I was a child again playing with friends in the field, a stick of wood in my hand instead of a real sword. That was the moment I realised I was actually holding the sword. I could touch and feel some things.

I hadn't finished searching but I had to tell Trinity. I could come back later to finish looking. I quickly replaced the sword and headed for the door. It opened and the maid returned. She walked past me; the door passed through me. The girl went back to the fireplace to straighten the vase she'd moved, turned around and left the room, passing the door over me once again as it closed. I followed her into the hall, spun round and went back into the drawing room – through the oak door. That was when I discovered I could walk through solid objects. I couldn't explain it but I could feel some solid things, such as the sword but others, like the door, I couldn't.

I ran up the main stairs, it didn't matter now; only the gods painted on the ceiling could see me and they couldn't tell me off. I knocked on the door of Trinity's room, calling her name. Without warning, her head came through the wall smiling at me.

'Did you know we could do this?' The rest of her appeared. 'Such good fun, don't you think?'

'That's what I came to tell you. Have you tried picking stuff up, you know like small things? I just had a go with Mr Washbury's sword.'

'No I haven't. Come in and show me,' she said, disappearing through the door.

I followed. I crossed the room to her bed table and picked up a book. Trinity tried a silver hairbrush and hand mirror from her dressing table.

'Oh, good, at last I can do my hair. It feels such a mess.' Bending to see herself in the mirror, she gulped. 'I'm not there. Albert, I've no reflection.' I joined her to look in the mirror. 'Oh, dear, oh dear. I'll have to brush it without looking. You can be my mirror, Albert; my maid. He he.'

I watched as Trinity tried making strokes. 'Sorry, miss, but nothing's happened. I think we have to stay as we are.'

She flopped back onto her counterpane. I noticed it didn't change shape and thought of something. I tried to push the dressing table chair. It didn't move. I decided later I would have to experiment.

I explained what Shadwick was up to and my efforts to find Lady Margaret's letter.

'And you didn't see what he did with it, miss?'

'Sorry, Albert. Maybe he simply slipped it in his pocket; so it is safe – in a way.'

'Miss Trinity, what do you think will happen to the house if . . . if Mr Washbury doesn't come back?'

A week later I had my answer.

I was sitting in the servant's hall doing nothing, of course. It was interesting to watch all comings and goings. It was where I felt most at home. I heard Trinity calling my name.

'Albert, there you are. I've been looking everywhere. Jacob, Daniel's brother is here; his carriage is arriving. He'll have news. Hurry along upstairs!'

We raced up to the hall where a portly young man in a travelling cloak was addressing Shadwick.

'. . . and then I should like to address the staff, Shadwick.'

'Myself, the cook and housekeeper, I assume, sir. The head gardener?'

'*All* the staff, man, *all* of them.' Mr Jacob took his bearings. 'This will be a suitable space. Tell cook a few cold cuts will do. Oh, and Shadwick, a glass of my brother's best claret, if you please.'

'Certainly, Mr Jacob. Er, your coat, sir?'

The man shrugged it off his shoulders without waiting for assistance. Shadwick left with it over his arm.

'He's very direct isn't he,' I said, watching him approach the sitting room.

'I don't really like him much. He's several years, three I think, younger than Daniel. It sounds as if he intends to tell everyone the news in one announcement.'

'We'll have to wait. Take a seat, miss, and I'll bring you a glass of Mr Daniel's best claret. That's if Shadwick's left any in the cellar.'

'He, he, If only you could, Albert.'

An hour later the staff assembled to hear their fate.

13

'Wow! Congrats to Rogerson for buying somewhere with a totally cool history. Well done, darling.' She leaned over and kissed him on the cheek. 'I'll just finish off this little bit from Plantagenet, shall I?'

Arathea continued. '"Mr Jacob Washbury, acting upon instructions from his brother in jail, had closed the house and released the staff with a generous settlement. It was six months before the case went to trial and a further six before the ultimate penalties were paid. Mr Jacob, the man whose hospitality I was enjoying, was bequeathed Ruddyard Park house, grounds and estate by his brother but did not take possession until 1880." Then there's more blah-de-blah about all the rooms, etcetera. Enough of that, I think.'

Carla asked, 'May I borrow the book for room descriptions. It will be big help for redecoration.'

With a nod from Kingsley, Arathea passed it across.

'Well done, Arathea,' said Zinnia, 'and no interruptions by the . . . ghosts and ghoulies.' Her green eyes, a family trait, twinkled with humour.

Carla looked around apprehensively.

'Not yet, madam,' said Trinity as she took my hand. 'Oh Albie, we haven't had so much fun in years. I've got another idea. Back to the drawing room.' As we entered, she continued, 'Let's see if we can make this picture cabinet work.'

We'd seen it showing moving paintings when it was delivered with the furniture: really noisy people dancing and shouting to strange music. Very vivid, flashing electric-city lights. I was embarrassed for Trinity watching men and women wearing hardly any clothes but she didn't seem to care. We were both too fascinated by the colourful images, I think.

'The workmen had a short black stick with coloured beads stuck on one side. Can you see it anywhere? They pressed the beads to summon the pictures.'

'This thing? What shall I do with it? There are red and green beads on top like on the . . . phone,' she giggled at the unfamiliar word, 'I'll try those.'

We watched the front of the box, polished like black lacquer. At first nothing happened then suddenly there was a painting of a serious-looking man staring at us. He looked as if he was about to berate us for touching things without asking first. Then he spoke.

'To win five thousand pounds tell me in what year Stevenson's Rocket was built?'

'It was made in 1829 in Newcastle-upon-Tyne,' answered Trinity. 'Daniel taught me that.'

I hugged her. 'You're rich! The man's going to give you five thousand pounds!' I jumped up and down in my excitement before realising what I was doing. 'Sorry, sorry! I got carried away.'

'Honestly, Albert! That is no way for a servant to carry on with his master's fiancée. He, he; only teasing. I wonder how I receive the money.' She spoke over the man in the box who was still talking.

'Perhaps you touch one of the other beads. Try the number five for five thousand.'

The man disappeared to be replaced by coloured drawings of animals such as children might make with their crayons except these were moving and talking to each other in odd squeaks and squawks.

'Isn't it clever. When our visitors depart do you think they'll leave this behind? We could have lots of fun with it whatever it's called.'

Zinnia's voice came from behind us. 'I told you I could hear the television. Look.'

Trinity and I tried out the new word. 'Tellyvision.'

'You're right Auntie, someone's switched it on. Oh my goodness!' Arathea caught her breath as she pointed at us. 'The remote! It's floating in mid-air!'

'Remote?' Trinity looked at her hand in surprise then immediately dropped the beaded stick. It bounced on the carpet.

Carla stood behind her. 'Now you believe. Spirits are here. We need séance.'

She crossed the room to where we stood like children caught in the act of doing something naughty. She knelt to pick up the 'remote' thing, only inches from our feet. As she stood with it tightly in her hand she closed her eyes, breathing deeply before she spoke.

'I know you're here,' she whispered so quietly no-one but us could hear. 'I am friend.'

'Better get that TV checked out,' said Nutball, 'must be faulty.'

'Teevee,' we mumbled to each other.

'No faulty,' said Carla with a child-scolding voice. 'Look.' She pressed the beads to bring changing pictures to the box.

Rogerson spoke. 'I think Carla is right. We'll have a séance. Not today, let's all just settle in. Perhaps tomorrow evening Carla?' She nodded her agreement. He looked at his phone box. 'It's a little early but why don't we all relax with a drink on the terrace. Carla, would you mind?'

'Of course, sir. At the moment easier to go through front door because of the works in the saloon. Sorry for inconvenience, Mr Lovatt – and,' she looked shyly at him, 'thank you for supporting me.'

'Don't apologise, Carla, you've achieved wonders with this place. How about a bottle of something fizzy, eh everyone? Join us Carla, please.'

'Lovely idea, darling,' said Arathea.

'Scotch, soda, ice,' said the doctor. No please or thank you, I noticed. Mr Lovatt is much more polite.

Carla muttered something about spirits.

Trinity and I agreed to follow the group out onto the terrace where they sat around a new white wrought-iron table on matching cushioned chairs.

'There's an old drawing somewhere showing how the original garden once looked. Carla probably has it; she's organising the gardeners,' said Rogerson waving his arm towards the dusty, scrubby space. 'It was beautiful.'

Arathea was helping her aunt, adjusting the chiffon scarf tying back her long red hair.

'Such a shame it was allowed to go to rack and ruin,' said Zinnia.

'It doesn't look that bad, Auntie,' Arathea said with a smile, stroking Zinnia's tresses.

'Not my hair, silly! The garden. How do these things happen?'

'Well in Jacob Washbury's case it was poor management,' Rogerson explained. 'He didn't want to take on Ruddyard Park in the first place which is why it remained empty for ten years as we heard from Arathea. He knew it was beyond him, something in which he was proved right eventually. The debt climbed, he sold off land and farms. Then he sold off quite a lot of furniture. Luckily for me, one thing he was good at was record-keeping so when I tasked my chaps with tracking it down, their lives were made much easier. His ledgers were retained by the state and they couldn't have been more helpful to us. More debt, more sales. And so it went on until perhaps half the estate had gone. Eventually it was passed to the Crown as they were the major creditor.'

Extract from peace.warman.blog. Posted 02.05.2012

Next time you're stately home spotting, flicking the glossy pages of Country Life in the hairdresser or in the doctors' waiting room, or taking the 11.00 tour in a National Trust manor house, spare a thought for how the old place might have looked seventy years ago. In plenty of cases, not quite so grand. There was a war on.

These places have always adapted as fashions or ways of living changed. For instance, following the First World War, many could no longer afford the large staff they once had and countless maids and footmen no longer desired a career in service. Thus, the landowners had to adjust.

During WWII, one role which a lot of houses took on was that of hospital. Houses were requisitioned by the government on a lease from the owners as military hospitals or as civilian replacements for urban hospitals which it was feared would be bombed. A significant number of those owned by the Crown were leased to the Americans. In each theatre of operations, fixed hospitals operated in what was called the "Communications Zone (COMZ)." In the European Theatre, that was originally in England. The US military began setting up hospitals in a big way in 1942-43. Why? Then it was Top Secret. Now we know it was part of the plan for what would popularly become known as D-day.

different: clothes, accents, language, the equipment they brought with them. It was as if they had stepped from the pages of a fantasy tale.

Firstly, a group of men in brown coveralls arrived to shift the furniture or what there was left of it. We hadn't seen or heard them coming as we were out in the fields. We returned to find an odd-looking van at the front door. It had strange small fat wheels and there were no horses; we assumed they must have been left at the old stables. Same with the paintings. As much as possible was crammed in the drawing room; it took ten of them to move the dining table; it was so big and heavy. All the carpets were rolled and stacked in there; replaced with a sort of thick hessian matting, but they left the drapes at the windows.

Iron bedsteads, mattresses and bedding were delivered to the saloon and sitting room and set up in rows. After the shifters had removed the books other men put beds in the library and some in the hall as well. All together there were thirty-six beds to begin with. The study was left as an office for the man-in-charge: Colonel English. What we called the day room, a small space where Lady Margaret used to sit and sew because the light was good, was where eventually the surgeons carried on their gruesome business; cutting and sewing of a different kind. Men sometimes died in there which was perhaps a relief for them going by some of the screams we used to hear.

Once the beds had been set up, all sorts of bottles and pipes and stands and bowls arrived along with boxes and crates of other equipment.

This was followed by men and women we realised later were the doctors and nurses who began sorting it out.

It was the night they arrived Trinity and I realised we had a problem. I'd become used to sleeping in the master's bedroom; it would have been a shame to let it go to waste. Trinity, of course, had always slept in her own room.

I was exhausted from watching the lifting and carrying activity. Even so, I wished I could join in and help them. As I stood at the foot about to flop backwards onto the bed, there was a scream from next door. Trinity. I raced through the wall to her aid. She was quaking in the middle of the room.

14

'There's a m-man in my b-bed, Albie! Do something!'

I was at a loss. 'What do you want me to do, miss? I can't tell him off or shoo him out; he won't hear me.'

She stopped flapping. 'I wish we were the haunting type of ghosts then we could run around going woo-ooo, woo-ooo!'

'How do we know we're not? We've never tried it. Have a go now.'

She laughed as she called, 'Woo-ooo, woo-ooo! He, he. I sound like a sick owl.'

'Like a sick ol' what?'

'Pardon. Oh, I get it. Um, right, like a sick oul' ghoul?'

'Very good, Trinity. That's the spirit! Ha, ha!'

She groaned. 'Yes, good fun, Albie but what are we going to do?'

'There's plenty of bedrooms in this house just along the landing. Take your pick.'

'You can't say *there's*, or *there is*, because the following noun: bedrooms, is plural so you must say: *there are* bedrooms.'

'Oh, Trinity, do stop that!'

'Can I sleep in your bed, pleeease . . .' she said in her little girl voice.

She flustered me. 'I beg your pardon! I-I-I . . . . I'm flattered you would want . . . to . . . you know. After all this time of knowing each other.' I

130

smoothed my hair. 'I mean, I don't know what to say.'

'. . . and then you can find another room. It is such a comfortable bed. And I am the mistress of the house in a manner of speaking.'

'Oh! Yes, of course. I knew that's what you meant. Well, I suppose so but we'll have to sort something out in the morning.' I turned to the wall behind her bed. 'I'll try this way then. G'night.'

I was half-way through the wall when she shrieked again. I rushed to my room.

'Albie, Albie! There's another man in my bed!'

'This is a very inconvenient habit you're developing, Miss Trinity. Anyway, to be accurate: there's a man in *my* bed, not yours. He was sitting up looking around trying to ascertain where the sound came from.

'I think he heard you. Look, it's the Colonel. He must have decided to take this room. And that's probably the Captain next door.'

'Hmph. To be truly precise, Albert, there's a man in *Daniel's* bed. So there.'

'So, as we are being correct; you're the mistress of the house, so you get rid of him. I'm going to find somewhere to sleep. So there!'

I stormed off back through her room where I'd been heading to the one beyond. I don't know how long after I'd arrived in the bedroom that someone slapped my face.

'Albert Hapless! Stop staring and close your mouth! What would Lizzie think of you? Shameful!'

When I'd walked in, I was stopped in my tracks, mesmerised. Four chattering, giggling young ladies in various states of undress were sitting or standing as they laid clothing on the two large beds from small valises. They wore the smallest drawers I'd ever seen, no corsets, only a sort of top to cover their . . . modesty. Legs were fully on show. I had never seen such a quantity of female skin. I was thinking how soft, white and curvy it looked, imagining . . . . And that's when the clout almost knocked my block off. My cheek burnt.

'Albie! You're opening and closing your mouth and no sound is coming out. You look like a fish. Avert your eyes!'

Another smack on the other side of my face. I turned my head to focus on my attacker.

'Trinity! Stop hitting me. If I wasn't a ghost my cheeks would be bright red instead of pale and rosy as they usually are.'

'From embarrassment I hope! Such reprehensible behaviour. We're leaving.' She grabbed my hand, dragging me through the wall into the next bedroom.

'Oh no! Don't look, Albie. Come with me.'

I peeped. More girls. One was actually . . . . My arm was yanked almost from its socket.

'I said, *don't* look!'

'Did you see what they were wearing, Trinity?'

'Or *not* wearing, Albie!'

We stood in the passage, doors on either side.

All I could think to say was, 'Um.'

'Now, it looks as if we aren't going to be sleeping along here tonight. The staff have commandeered the bedrooms. Where are the servant's quarters? We'll have to sleep there. Lead on Macduff.'

I smiled to myself. Of all the books I'd read in the library, Shakespeare's were my favourites. I'd read his plays countless times. After all these years I was going to get my own back and put Trinity right.

I faced her, hands on hips, trying to look assertive. 'Actually, the correct quotation from Mr Shakespeare's Macbeth is, "*Lay* on, Macduff, and damned be him who first cries 'Hold! enough!'"

'Never mind that. Please lead the way, Albie.'

She flapped her hand in front of me.

'We'll check the bedrooms properly tomorrow morning to see if any are unoccupied but for tonight you'll have to sleep like a servant on a small hard bed.'

I said that tongue in cheek, knowing it didn't make the slightest difference to us where we slept; hard, soft or even a bed of nails were all the same to a ghost. The comfort was all in our heads.

We wound our way along the back corridor and staircase. There had never been carpet here; servants didn't need such luxury, only bare floorboards. I recalled a few occasions when I'd had to run this route in the middle of the night, summoned from my sleep to help a drunken Sir George who'd fallen from his bed.

'Gosh, these passages are very narrow aren't they. How on earth did a woman pass through here with her crinoline?'

I laughed. 'Servants don't wear such things, Trinity. Members of the household, or their guests, crinolined or be-suited, never passed that door back there.'

'I will accompany you tomorrow, Albie, to ensure you do not take surreptitious peeks at the young girls.'

'As if—'

'I saw you.'

'Please don't tell Lizzie. Here we are. This is the housekeeper's room; it's larger and had a better bed. A window as well. In you go. I'm next door in the butler's old room.'

We separated until the morning.

I opened one eye to peer at the sky through the window; not that the weather made any difference to Trinity or me; we don't get wet so rain doesn't trouble us. Outside was pale, pre-dawn grey. I wondered what the Americans made of the English climate. Was it much different to their own?

I lay, staring at the peeling paint on the ceiling, thinking about the days when I dreamed of this being my room, when I finally achieved the position of butler. I was certain I'd be better than Shadwick. Me with Lizzie as housekeeper running the whole place. Everything would have been perfect – happy upstairs and down. I closed my eyes, picturing Lizzie's smiling face, her dark eyes and long, black hair. I realised I'd seen more of those nurses than I had of my own beloved. As I drifted into sleep, it made me wonder what my Lizzie wore under her cotton dress. From what I recalled of such garments swaying on the washing line, it was a lot more than the nurses.

Scratch, scratch.

My eyes popped open. I turned my head to the window, then the door.

Scratch, scratch.

I sat up, looking around the room: bare walls, simple floorboards left for years without polish, no furniture. Even the cobwebs had cobwebs.

Another scraping sound had me looking at the floor beneath the window. I was about to turn away when something moved.

'Hello, little fellow, what are you up to?'

A tiny black nose and quivering whiskers stared back at me. The mouse's little legs scampered along the skirting board to the corner and back before stopping and gazing at me once more. I could see the floorboard joints through its body.

'Are you a ghost mouse?' I asked as I swung my legs out of bed.

It ran over my shoe, up my hose and breeches leg to sit on my knee. It tipped its head this way and that examining my face as its nose and whiskers twitched. I'm sure it smiled.

'I've never met a ghost mouse before. Shame you can't speak.' I lowered my voice. 'Make a change from Trinity.'

'What would make a change from Trinity?'

Without turning about, I said, 'Don't you knock when you enter a gentleman's room?'

She ignored my question. 'Who were you talking to about me?'

My new friend had disappeared. 'I-I was praying for you . . . for us. Please take the fetters from my ankles and the chains from Trinity.'

'Oh, metaphors. Well done, Albie. Do you know what a metaphor is?'

'Um, one more than a meta-three?' She tutted. 'Come on Trinity, let's go bedroom hunting, shall we?'

Just because we awoke early didn't mean the Americans did the same.

'I'll look in the ladies' rooms; you try the men's,' Trinity ordered.

The same four bedrooms were occupied which left six more to check.

'We'll take three each, and Albie,' she wagged a finger, 'if there are any girls you come straight back and report to me.'

I saluted. 'Yes, Commander. And the same if you find any men – or I'll tell Mr Daniel.'

It looked as if two might be taken even though there was no-one sleeping in them. Each of the beds had a travelling case on it. The other rooms appeared to be vacant but the beds had been stored on their sides. It made me sad remembering when every room was full at weekends.

'Hmn, I think we'll have to come back tonight after everyone's gone to bed,' I suggested. 'Did you sleep comfortably?'

'Tolerably well.'
'Good. You might have to get used to it.'

15

Our attention was taken suddenly by shouting and rumbling noises outside. Trinity disappeared through the floor whilst I jumped down the main staircase to the front door. Our first shock was the horseless carriages and wagons coming down the drive; some were like the ones used by the furniture shifters we'd seen. These were dark green. White squares painted on the sides contained a red cross.

'How are they moving? It's like magic. Are the horses hidden inside? I can't see any legs.'

'They're like Daniel's engines only smaller, so they must be driven by steam like his trains, although I don't see any smoke. Isn't it clever, Albie?'

Men in dull green uniforms ran alongside the vehicles, some hung on the sides near the front. Others ran in and out of the house, shouting instructions to one another. More followed carrying portable canvas beds on poles; blankets of the same dull green covered the men. Several men in white coats rushed from the door to greet soldiers alighting the wagons.

'Those are the physicians. Here come the patients.'

We couldn't help ourselves. We stood on the terrace gawping at the men trudging or being carried across the drive. A few of them used crutches or other soldiers for support. Most were wrapped in bloody bandages: heads, arms, legs. Many of the ones being carried had lost a leg. The last ones walked past chatting and I was certain two of them waved to us but realised they couldn't have done.

'Oh, Albie, those poor young fellows are in a terrible state – blinded, crippled and, worst of all, missing limbs. It's like our armless army all those years ago except these men are still alive. War is a terrible thing.'

After a while we returned to the house passing the Colonel as he strode out to greet the soldiers. Once again we gaped, this time at the spectacle of the electric-city lights shining in every room.

'Oh my goodness, doesn't it all look so different. Look at the paintings on the hall stairs and ceiling. Beautiful.'

Electric-city was one of the many things Mr Jacob wasted his money on. I think it was the fashion in the big houses, installed to impress visitors. Our house continued using candles everywhere even after it was fitted.

'I haven't seen the old place looking so bright for forty or more years.'

It turned out the Americans brought their own electric-city with them in noisy, smelly engines which somehow made the lights work. They weren't steam though. Generators, they called them.

The nurses were up and about now in smart grey-green uniforms with little hats covering the top of their hair, scurrying from room to room, bed to

I took her hand and led her out of the saloon.

A nurse walked through Trinity and turned the same knob. The lively music returned.

'Let's look around,' I suggested. 'And please don't touch anything. Promise?'

She looked sulky. 'Alright.'

Passing along the line of beds in the hall, I released her hand as we followed the Colonel walking briskly through, nodding at the men. Trinity was obviously in one of her childish moods as she fell in behind him, marching and swinging her arms. I knew she was trying to get me to laugh to make up for touching the radio. It worked.

We followed the Colonel to what used to be Mr Daniel's study from where I could hear ringing; not one bell like those in the servant's hall but like all of them at once. The sound came from an odd-shaped black box with a large handle on top. It sat on the corner of the desk next to another one. He grabbed the handle and it broke off. The noise stopped.

'See,' said Trinity, 'I'm not the only one who breaks things.'

'The difference is he probably knows how to mend it.'

'Hello!' The Colonel was talking to one end of the handle with the other end pressed to his ear.

'Look, Albie, it's got a wire so it's something else made of electric-city.'

'Yes, this is Southern Base Section, Colonel English speaking. Sure thing, Major, good to know. Yep, yep. Fill me in later.'

The Colonel banged the handle down and hurried from the room. Dangerous. Trinity's arm snaked towards the desk.

'No! You promised.'

'But it's already broken so I can't hurt it, can I? And it looks so interesting.'

'Trinity,' I used my fierce face and warning voice, 'do *not* touch.'

She touched. It jangled. She jumped back. Straight through the Captain who was walking in the door. He picked up the handle.

'Captain Chadwick.'

I turned to Trinity. 'W-what did he say?' I reached out for her to steady me.

'I don't think it was Shadwick; more like ch for Chadwick.'

'Uh-huh, uh-huh.' The Captain waved to someone behind me. 'I'll get the Colonel.'

'Made me go all faint.'

'You are faint, Albie, I can see right through you! He, he.'

I shivered as a nurse stepped into me and faced the Captain.

'Nurse, can you find the Colonel and tell him HQ's on the line. Pronto.'

The young lady ignored me as she left. I shivered again.

Next it was Trinity's turn as the Colonel appeared in the room to take the black handle from the other man who then exited through Trinity.

'Let's go and watch from the stairs again,' I said, wanting to get her away from new objects she could break.

sleeping quarters he said he'd find somewhere to "bunk down" later.

Back in the butler's room I was greeted by my new friend sitting on the bed. He scampered up and down in excitement when I arrived. I sat next to him, putting out my hand. He jumped into my palm, ran up my arm, across my shoulders and down the other arm which made me chuckle. Next, he leapt from the bed to the floor, disappearing into the corner. I couldn't see him anywhere so assumed he'd gone to bed for the night. I lay down and did the same.

A minute later I heard him scratching and looked to the corner. He ran along the floorboards and disappeared. I knelt for a closer look. Up against the skirting a knot had fallen from one of the short end-pieces of board leaving a mouse-sized hole. I smiled at the thought of him making a little cosy home for himself. He popped out of the cavity, ran to me then back down as if he was performing. He did it again.

'You want me to play a game?'

The third time he appeared with a scrap of something in his little mouth, dropping it in front of me. It was a corner of a sheet of paper. He scampered back once more then sat with his nose and whiskers poking out.

'Do you want me to come to your house, is that it?'

I edged nearer. He ducked inside. I put my finger in the hole and pulled. The board was about nine inches long and came away easily like a lid. Mousey jumped out and watched as I put my hand inside to lift out a cloth pocket stuffed with letters and newspaper cuttings.

16

Jeremiah Shadwick! You fraud!'

Trinity isn't the only person with an inquisitive nature. I had unfolded the notepaper sheets, seven in all. Each contained the same few sentences written in almost the same hand. Except for the last one which was a complete letter. My eyes remained fixed on it for several minutes.

I was so excited by my discovery I almost burst through the wall into Trinity's room to tell her. That was before I read the newspaper cuttings. They gave me something extra to think about. It had never occurred to either of us that anyone in the house had been involved in the plot which had got us killed but the yellow newsprint in my hand made me think again.

Why would Shadwick have collected information on Oddfellow and Bristler?

Going by the dates on the papers he was interested in them several months *before* the plot. Why? I could understand his reading information about them afterwards out of simple curiosity, but beforehand? It didn't make sense unless . . . .

I had often wondered about the coincidence of the servants being out of the way on the night. Very convenient. Also, who gave entrance to the men? And who had tipped off the preacher? Now I began to wonder if Shadwick was in on it. He went to London on occasion. He went to the church like everyone else; I'd heard him say he liked the new vicar, unlike most of the congregation. He held the keys to the house. He knew Mr Daniel's movements.

I tucked the papers back under the floorboards with mousey on sentry duty and drifted off to sleep; all those loose ends flapping around like the reeds on one of my mum's partly-woven baskets. If she were here, I'd ask her what to do. She'd say, do what you think is right Albie. Now I only had Trinity. She'd want to make an adventure from it. I wondered if I could talk it over with my little friend and find such a thing as ghost cheese for him.

In the morning I poked my head through the wall to see if Trinity was awake. She obviously was because the bed was empty. I went searching. After checking every room in the house and listening to the songs on the radio I was attracted by the activity outside. A dozen or more soldiers were struggling against wind and rain to erect a large marquee on the front lawn. Unlike the crisp white ones used by Sir George and Lady M for summer luncheon parties this was an ugly shade of green painted with brown patches. If it's for a party I said to myself, it'll be a very dull affair. After an hour I found Trinity outside in the driveway sitting in the rear compartment of one of the wagons, shamelessly laughing and giggling, surrounded by men.

'Ahem!' was all I could think to say as I peered into the gloomy interior.

Trinity greeted me. 'We're sheltering from the rain, Albie. Didn't want to *dampen our spirits*! He, he, he!'

'Well, is that a fact. Tell you what Al, I sure could look after the needs of—'

I jumped to my feet. 'How dare you!'

'Kirk!' Ahab's voice was commanding.

'Sit down, Albie, he's only joking,' said Trinity. 'They've all promised to try to find the right department upstairs,' she raised her eyes to heaven, 'to tell them of our innocence. I told the guys; that's American for chaps, we'd show them the grounds. Come on everyone, let's go.'

I climbed down; the soldiers enjoyed the novelty of jumping through the canvas sides of the wagon, or truck as they called it. As we walked, the novice ghosts played around like children, doing the things only the spirits can do: walking through people and objects. Kirk struggled to walk with his legs bound hip to toe. He managed with a side-to-side twisting motion. Sam found he was able to levitate like Trinity so would suddenly disappear only to reappear on top of a building or tree.

Whilst Trinity explained how a parterre garden was built and planted with different species for each bed, I learned about how the horseless carriages worked. Such a clever invention. I also talked to Kirk who, underneath his coarse exterior, was a nice man, always making a joke of everything.

'Doc said don't tell anyone what happened to my legs,' he said with a wink, patting the bandages, 'it's a secret. Says I gotta keep it under wraps. Ha, ha!'

He tried to explain the workings of the radio to me – "you Limeys call it a wireless" – but I found it difficult to understand how the sound travelled through the air. Another ingenious idea. He had to translate "Limeys" for me.

Grover was the opposite; a serious man. He explained about the German corporal named Hitler who wanted to take over the world and the British Prime Minister, a Mr Churchill, who wanted to stop him. We agreed it must be in the German nature; I told him about Mr Bismarck invading Denmark.

Chester left the group and returned to the house. When he found us an hour later he told us he'd been visiting a friend who was able to see and talk to him. His theory was that, as his friend was dying, he was on his way to being a ghost and therefore they could communicate. This intrigued the others so they left to investigate. Sam took Chester to find his arms. Trinity and I sat quietly. The sudden silence affected her.

'Oh, Albie, it's so nice to have other people around, isn't it?'

'Sure thing honey,' I said mimicking Kirk.

'Good to see you absorbing the vernacular, or "lingo" as they say, buddy.'

'Strange language, isn't it? Funny thing is, they think they're speaking pure English.'

With all the excitement of meeting new friends I'd forgotten the reason for wanting to find Trinity earlier.

'Come with me, I've something to show you. It's in the butler's room.'

We hurried to the house. I negotiated the beds in the hall; I didn't want to walk through all those people, then climbed the stairs. Trinity floated through the ceiling. I found her sitting on my bed.

'I wish you wouldn't do that vertical thing, it's very disconcerting.'

'You're just jealous. What have you got?' She jumped up. 'Eek! A mouse! Shoo, shoo!'

My new friend had climbed onto the bed to say hello.

'Don't be like that.' I held out my hand; he climbed aboard. 'This is Mousey; he found what I'm going to show you. He's a ghost, like us.'

'Aah, I didn't realise. Isn't he sweet,' she said, putting her hand next to mine.

I retrieved the cloth pocket from beneath the floor and handed it to Trinity. 'I think these might help us to understand what happened on our Deathday.' We read them together, incomplete letters first then the final one.

Rackingham Manor, Bassett-next-Sinstone, Buckinghamshire

To whom it may concern.

The bearer of this letter, one Jeremiah Shadwick, has been in the employ of this family for many years. He has performed his duties as first footman and latterly as butler, in exemplary fashion. He is of the highest calibre, a man of integrity: trustworthy and conscientious. He is much liked by the family and the remainder of the servants.

It is with regret that, due to family considerations, The Manor must be sold and the household dispersed, hence Shadwick's departure from our service.

I commend him highly to any future employer.

With God's grace,

Sir William Rackingham

'This is a forgery, Albie! What a disgrace! You can see he was practising his handwriting with these others.'

'That's exactly what I thought. Sir William Rackingham, if indeed he exists, did not write this letter of character. Shadwick was a fraud. Now look at the newspaper articles, especially the handwritten dates.'

June 27
VANDALS ATTACK PARLIAMENT

Notorious dissenters, Mr Bertram Oddfellow and Mr Toby Bristler, yesterday caused a public affray at 1.10 pm at The Palace of Westminster by hurling stones through the Palace windows with no regard for the safety of those within.

"These men are nothing more than vandals," one indignant Member of Parliament said to our reporter. "They should be locked up but they were given no more than a warning."

The men were protesting Mr Gladstone's latest housing bill.

July 3rd
ODDFELLOW THREATENS PM

As Mr Gladstone strolled away from 10 Downing Street, *SW* accompanied by two ministers he was verbally set upon by one Bertram Oddfellow of Islington, *N* railing the Prime Minister and his "Parliamentary Cronies" were unfit for office and that policies made by "decrepit, old men" were disastrous for the average worker. A bystander who wrestled him to the ground reported Mr Oddfellow shouted in Mr Gladstone's face, "You are close to your grave, sir!"

Later, Mr Oddfellow told our newspaper, "I was referring to Mr Gladstone's age taking him closer to his grave, not threatening to put him there!"

Bertram Oddfellow is often in the company of other agitators, most notably a Mr Toby Bristler of Hackney, *E*, a known reformer and objector. Both have recently been campaigning against the nationalisation of the railways.

July 5
MR OUTLANDISH: RAILWAYS PROPOSAL
This Newspaper's Opinion

Mr James Outlandish is a man of means; owner of a large country estate, employer of many household servants and tied workers on his tenanted farms. He is a

Member of Parliament who, we are reliably informed, attends to his duties at the Palace of Westminster on two or three occasions each month. Sources local to his rural home advise this journal he spends much of his time at leisure.

One wonders, therefore, why a man so evidently not of the working class has chosen to propose a Bill for the nationalisation of the railways – *for the good of the people*.

"*The* power over so much of the population by so few self-styled 'industrialists' such as Mr Royston Gosport and Mr Daniel Washbury for instance, who line their pockets with the half-pennies of the workers is a disgrace," he says. This columnist would like to ask Mr Outlandish if he has ever seen a half-penny or asked any of his staff what they would be able to purchase with one.

At least some of these 'industrialists' to whom he refers arrived at their current situations from less privileged backgrounds than he and may have actually felt the weight of a half-penny in their pocket at one time.

This newspaper is of a mind to question Mr Outlandish's sincerity in this venture – but not in his other stated endeavour: to be a future Prime Minister – *for the good of the people*.

July 20th
'PRINCES' AGAINST
OUTLANDISH

- It has become the custom in Parliament Square, Westminster, *SW*, for gangs of ruffians, there is no better term for them, to appear each time Members of Parliament arrive and depart the Palace of Westminster. These men, led by the notorious pair: Toby Bristler and Bertram Oddfellow, jostle and shout abuse at the Right Honourable gentlemen without sense of decorum or concern for passers-by. Only yesterday our reporter personally escorted several ladies away from the scene to avoid their witnessing such boorish behaviour.

- For several weeks, led by Messrs Bristler and Oddfellow, they have been noisily demanding an end to the debates on the acquisition of the railways by the government.

- To the consternation of many, it appears they are not breaking any law and are within their rights as citizens and electors to have their say.

- When asked who they represented, Bristler told our correspondent, "We are the Princes of the Public. We speak on behalf of all hard-working and right-minded men: labourers and industrialists, rich and poor, demanding a government which will serve the interests of all the people, all the time."

- In a general statement to the press they stated: "Everything must be done to prevent such a catastrophe. Outlandish must be stopped *by any means*."

'Well, what do you think, Trinity?'

'Our butler doesn't seem to have been the upright citizen he had us believe. The way he practised the letter is exactly how we used to do it at school; imitating our teachers' handwriting to give our parents glowing reports on what clever little ladies we were.'

'I'm shocked at you!'

Mousey sat on her knee looking up at her face. He looked appalled too.

'Ah, now, is it my act of forgery that shocked you or is it me, the forger, which has shocked you. If it is then shocked *by* would be—'

'Stop it!'

'But . . . . Don't worry, Albie, our parents weren't convinced. It was only a game. But in Shadwick's case, it was more than that. The dates on the cuttings suggest he knew the names of Bristler and Oddfellow long before Daniel did. This is what I think.

'Shadwick was obviously a schemer; the letter proves that. My theory is he learned about those men from the newspapers and saw a way of making money. Somehow he approached them; although I'm not sure how a country butler would contact such men in London, and offered them access to Daniel and the house in return for payment. He was aware of the proximity of James Outlandish's estate to ours and knew they would be interested.'

'You think he suggested the murder?' I said, realising I'd been holding my hand over the bullet hole.

'Oh, I doubt that. No, I imagine he saw this house as somewhere nearby from where they could make mischief. These articles show the sort of troublemakers these fellows were; I imagine the assassination was their idea. Certainly not Daniel's.'

'I think you're right. I can't see Mr Daniel colluding with a butler as an accomplice to murder. We must keep these papers hidden; but where?'

'Put them back where you found them, Albie. They've been safe there for about seventy years so no reason they won't be secure for a further seventy.'

17

I was sitting on the stairs watching the comings and goings of our visitors. At breakfast they had confirmed to each other they had slept well on their first night. Even Nutball had congratulated Carla on her choice of mattress. Rogerson Lovatt had settled himself in the sitting room with a flat silver-coloured attaché case which had a smaller version of a television inside the lid. It had rows of letters and numbers on the base which made me think of another clever American invention we had seen; something called a typewriter. There was one in the Colonel's office. Trinity pushed some of the buttons on it one day and broke it. I could never begin to imagine what she must have been like as a child.

Miss Arathea and her auntie had gone for a walk across the fields. Trinity had joined them; she needed female company. It was a fine sunny April day like the ones we always used to have in July when the funfair came to the village green. It might rain the day before or the night it closed but the weather was always beautiful on fair days themselves.

I sat trying to imagine what it was like now. I wondered if it had grown into a town. People used to say London was a hamlet once upon a time. Was it still there? My dad used to say the red clay wouldn't last forever. Once this house closed, it must have destroyed a few of the merchants who used to deliver our supplies. Did the fair still come?

Did the George and Dragon still cover itself in flags of every colour on St Thomas's day? Did the boys still ride the carousel trying to entice the girls to sit two-to-a-horse? Did they still try to impress their girlfriends by hooping a prize on the hoop-la stall? I thought of the day I met my Lizzie there. Best day of my life.

Carla walked through me. I shivered. She turned around to look at the stairs. She definitely sensed Trinity and me. Today she was wearing black as usual, not a dress this time but trousers and a silky blouse. The clothing emphasised her slimness and height. She headed for Nutball who was sitting on one end of the large settle reading a book. Carla sat in the corner at the other end facing him. She plumped a cushion. He ignored her.

'Why you not like me, Mr Nutball?' she asked.

He looked up. 'Who said I didn't? And it's Doctor not Mister. Or if we're being sociable, Kingsley.' He closed his book to examine her.

'You are always . . . , what is English word? Curt. Yes, you are curt with me. Not polite. Not friendly like others, like Mr Lovatt.'

It sounded like the start of an interesting conversation so I went over to join them. I settled myself into one of the wing chairs, stroking the new plush upholstery.

'Carla, I'm not polite to anyone; haven't you noticed?' He's right there, I thought.

'Except Zinnia,' she muttered to herself. 'Defence mechanism. You are insecure. How does

that make you feel? Do you want to talk about it?'
she said.

'I-I . . . how do you know about such things?
You sound like a psychiatrist.'

'I know much.'

'Anyway, it's not you – personally. It's what
you've been talking about; ghosts and spirits and all
that mumbo-jumbo. I'm a very down-to-earth
person; it's my job. Why do you believe that stuff?'

'I grew up with it. Romania is a country full
of folklore, especially Transylvania – and not only
Dracula, before you make the jokes. You read many
books. Buy some about this; they will help in your
work.' The doctor stuttered an objection but she
continued. 'Like all myth: Greek, Roman, Celtic,
Inuit, South American, you name it, the stories are
based on need to explain what is happening in
world around. Why it rains? Depend where you are
– ask Zeus or Dodola. Why my crop fail? Ask Ceres
or Demeter or Pachamama. Why my mother die?
We say Strigoloi take her blood and make it bad.
Same story, different country.' Carla smiled. Her
normally sad face lit up with the enjoyment of her
subject and she became quite pretty. 'In big country
stories fade away. In mountains, always there.
Always believe.'

She sat up straighter. Nutball turned slightly
towards her. She kept the smile.

'Everybody talk to the dead. But with some
people the dead talk back. This was my
grandmother. She talks all the time with dead from
village. Everyone come to her; "Cici," her name,
"talk to my husband, please, ask him what I should

do." "Cici, ask my mother if I can marry this girl." Things like this. My mother did the same. I can do it sometimes but only if everyone helps me. I heard my first voices when I was a girl nine-years old.' Carla put out her hand to indicate the height of a young girl.

Nutball sat forward, removing his spectacles. I think people hearing voices in their head was his subject. This conversation was most interesting; I couldn't wait to tell Trinity.

'I was at school. The lesson was very boring about politics. A month earlier one boy had drowned in the lake; very sad. Suddenly, I heard him speak to me and stood up in the middle of class and said, "Peter says can we go to the lake sometimes to see him; he gets lonely." The teacher didn't question me. The kids said nothing. They knew my mother and grandmother, so if Carla said she heard Peter speaking, then she did and that was that. Next day we went to see him and he told me thank you. I didn't hear him any more after. I learned spirits only talk if they need help, otherwise they leave us alone. I think our spirits in this house want to tell us something to help them.

'You must be curious to know about these things, aren't you? You are scientist. I mean, harpsichord didn't play itself, you know. TV didn't turn itself on. You saw remote control floating. Aren't you even a little bit interested?'

'We-ell . . . . Mildly, let's say.' He tugged on an ear lobe. 'Those things are puzzling I admit but . . . you see I'm of the breed that says if it can't be explained then it can't happen; a bit like religion.

And it's never happened to me. However, if our host says we have a séance, then that's what we do. It'll be fun.'

'Not fun, I assure you . . . Kingsley.' Carla stood, serious-faced once more. 'Much work to do.'

He sat staring at the seat as if she were still there, deep in thought. I went and sat in her place and looked straight in his face to see if I could work out what was going on in his mind but couldn't get past his flat expression. I liked to believe she had convinced him there was something in what she said but . . . . He spoke.

'What a load of garbage!' he said, shaking his head.

'Kingsley, darling,' called Zinnia from the door, vividly-coloured fabric billowing around her legs from the breeze. 'You ought to have joined us; it's wonderful outside in the fresh country air.'

His face broke out of its rumpled grump into a broad smile as he stood to welcome the ladies. He replaced his glasses. Trinity hovered in the background as the others met in the centre of the entrance hall for cheek-kissing. I noticed Zinnia's lasted somewhat longer than Arathea's. Trinity joined me on the settle.

'He has designs on her, I think,' I told Trinity, nodding in Zinnia's direction. 'You should have seen his smile when you all walked in.'

'You should have seen their smiles last night, Albie.' She winked. 'He, he, he.'

'What do you—'

'It wasn't only "designs" he had on Aunt Zinnia in her boudoir. He, he.'

'What did he have on then?'

Trinity spread her arms wide. 'Nothing!'

'But you just said . . . . Don't play riddles with me Trinity. You said . . . .' I saw from her face she was being naughty – that mischievous little girl look she has. I realised what she meant. 'Oh! Oh, I see. In her room? Well, well. And how do you know this, may I ask?'

'I just happened to be walking the corridors last night; Hypnos wouldn't visit me.'

'I surely hope not. Who is this Hypnos? When did he arrive?' Sometimes Trinity's behaviour is shocking. I told her firmly, 'There are no visitors allowed in servants' rooms – especially those of young ladies!'

'It's a saying, Albie. Hypnos was the Greek god of sleep.' She shook her head in exasperation. 'Anyway, I discovered the guests weren't sleeping either. On my way to . . . nowhere in particular, I saw the good doctor being admitted to Auntie's room.'

'Perhaps she was unwell?'

'Ye-es. My thoughts exactly. On the way back I heard a sound from Zinnia's room and I, um, I was concerned for her well being. So, I put my head through the door and saw . . . . No matter what I saw; you'll have to imagine that. A lady cannot possibly enter into such detail.'

'What "lady"? Where is this personage? A young woman who spies on the night-time activities of the guests is hardly a *lady*. And, if I may ask, miss, where were you on the "way to" and the "way back" from?'

'I don't wish to divulge that information.' She put a finger to her lips. 'Anyway, even if I hadn't seen anything, I learned every element of the encounter by listening to Zinnia telling Arathea during their walk. The things she told her niece were . . . incredible. Ladies have no decorum these days.'

'Look who's talking! The bedroom spy! You didn't answer my question.'

'Alright, alright. I was on my way to the master bedroom – where Daniel and I used to sleep. There, I've confessed. Satisfied?' That's actually two confessions, I thought. 'I went to . . . to . . . bring back happy memories. The decorators have been so clever; it's exactly as it used to be – trailing roses on the wallpaper, deep red drapes at the windows and the same beautifully-embroidered bedcover. It looked as romantic as the first time Daniel carried me in there. I wanted to watch Rogerson and Arathea and pretend it was *me* with *my* fiancé. But I couldn't stay more than a few moments; it made me cry. Oh, Albie, I miss him so much. You must miss Lizzie in the same way, don't you?'

'Yes I do . . . but I don't go spying on people's private moments. Anyway, Lizzie and I didn't, um, I mean we never, you know. She wanted to wait till we were married. She wasn't a *modern girl* like you,' I said, recalling different words Mrs Carter sometimes used to describe Trinity's approach to life.

I changed the subject and told her what I'd overheard between Carla and Kingsley. I summarised.

'So, firstly, she believes we exist; she seems to sense our presence. Secondly, she can talk to dead people; her mother and grandmother did the same. Third, she says spirits only talk to the living if they need something – like us. And she thinks we want to tell her how to help us. Isn't that wonderful? This is our first real chance in a hundred-and-fifty years, don't you see. We've asked other spirits to help us but that's come to nothing. Now we have the opportunity to get someone living to do it.'

'You're right, Albie. But, you know, I'm certain all the souls meant well.'

'The hags didn't.'

'No. But our old ghost friends, the soldiers, they were good chaps – even if they were Americans. Mind you, helping us was dependent on them telling those upstairs we were innocent but they were a band of young rogues, really. They may not have gone in that direction.' She raised her eyes to heaven at the same time as pointing her finger downwards.

I reflected on our time with the US Army. Trinity was right; they were good men but, freed from the constraints of the living world, they were determined to have a good time. I lost count of how many friends we made. The rate at which newcomers arrived and died was alarming. The medical staff worked so hard. We got to know the routine, and the 'lingo' as they called it. When ambulances arrived, triage officers sent patients to pre-op, medical, shock, or evacuation beds. Surgical teams worked twelve hours on, then twelve hours off

to save the soldiers. The first ghost group we met: Ahab, Chester, Grover, Kirk and Sam, remained "for the duration" as they used to say. When one of the soldiers died, they established themselves as the welcoming committee to SOS Regiment: The Spirits of Soldiers. They were on hand to provide advice to new recruits.

That was their responsible side. They also had NWP: Nurse Watch Patrol when they took turns at sitting in the nurses' quarters "checking they get to bed safely – and alone." That was Kirk's idea. Once Chester got used to having his arms working, he founded the Lost Property Department. He took great delight in hiding small items belonging to doctors and nurses in patients' beds or bandages. He once stole a pair of "nylons", which were like ladies' silk hose, and tucked them under a soldier's pillow which made everyone laugh including the doctors.

On their first Christmas Day in Ruddyard Park, the SOS recruited the assistance of one of the 'near-death' patients who'd recovered and was waiting to leave. He was still able to talk to the spirits. He announced to the other patients some magic tricks for their festive entertainment. On his command we moved objects, made them fly around, and once I practised my juggling skills with three empty tin mugs. I think the following Christmas was the best fun, though. Ahab got all the ghosts to dress up as ghosts. We found we could drape sheets over our heads to walk around the beds. If a soldier or nurse grabbed the sheet to see who it was, there was no-one there of course. Everyone was bewildered but roared with laughter.

Like the Civil War soldiers we had helped, the American ghosts had a rainbow-shimmering gold staircase to ascend when it was time for them to leave. It was behind one of the gazebos at the corner of what remained of the low-walled front garden. The men saluted the American flag which had flown in that corner since they arrived. The formal departure ceremony was conducted by Ahab and Sam inside the little building. Trinity and I always waited outside at the foot of the stairs to say our goodbyes and make our pleas for the soldiers to present our case to the senior officers at the Headquarters above the clouds. Without fail, they pledged to do what they could.

On the day the last ones left, we tried to follow them up the stairway to Heaven before it disappeared. We made it to the fifth step where we fell straight through to the ground in a disappointed heap.

Trinity interrupted my thoughts. 'Albie? Are you listening to me?'

'Sorry, I was lost in the past. Perhaps our guests can find where Lady Margaret's letter is; it must be in the house somewhere. They'll search if we persuade them to.'

'Yes, but where shall we tell them to look? We tried everywhere years ago but found nothing.'

'Be positive, Trinity. Remember, we've only *just* found Shadwick's papers. If we can make them believe our story, they'll want to look. Carla will make them. She'll feel duty bound to help us; it's the sort of person she is.'

'That's true. And we must tell them about that awful butler and where to find his forged letters.'

'Are you sure you don't know of any secret place Daniel would have used?'

She shook her head.

'Just think, we might soon see Lizzie and Daniel. Won't that be amazing?'

'As long as we go 'upstairs' . . . not down to the cellar!'

18

I don't remember the exact year but it was a few years following Mr Jacob's departure and the closure of Ruddyard Park. The new century had arrived so perhaps it was o-two or -three. What little furniture remained after he'd cleared his debts had gathered fluff as thick as a carpet. Lizzie would have been horrified; her duster losing ostrich feathers as she flicked everything in sight.

Jacob Washbury seemed a decent enough man. At twenty-nine he was three years younger than his brother when Daniel was arrested. His father had always supported him and when Daniel made his fortune he took over the role of Jacob's benefactor. So, by the time the younger Washbury took over the estate at the age of forty he'd never had to work in his life. By then he was married with daughters aged eleven and eight, both precocious and spoilt. Daniel's older sister Hermione, a rather masculine-looking lady, moved in with Jacob's family.

Suddenly, having had the place to ourselves for ten years, Trinity and I had a house full of people to avoid, and not just the family. The new Washburys loved to entertain. Almost every weekend the bedrooms were occupied by house visitors, party guests, shooting parties and long-lost relations. Extra staff were hired, the larders overflowed, local tradesmen rubbed their hands with glee at the growing orders from Ruddyard

Park. Those who could remember the Kingswoods' entertaining marvelled at how much money could be spent on food and drink.

Meals of seven, eight or nine courses were not unusual. Whilst much produce such as rabbit, veal, ham, beef, and game in season was sourced from the estate, the Washburys had exotic tastes. Oysters, lobster, salmon and other seafoods had to be purchased locally. Exotic fruits, sugar, molasses and chocolate arrived in local shops from London and Liverpool. Local retailers bought in beers from nearby Oxford or the Midlands and cider from Somerset and Herefordshire.

Jacob enjoyed playing the country gentleman. He rode around the estate calling upon his tenant farmers, always with a cheerful word despite the fact they owed rent and were fiddling the figures. It wasn't long before more money was being spent than was earned but Mr Jacob was slow in catching on. The debts began piling up. After many years, the Exchequer was owed more than everyone else's bills added together.

Trinity and I used to listen to the butler, housekeeper and estate manager grousing to each other over glasses of sherry in the butler's office. We'd shout at them.

'Go and tell him!'

'If you don't show him what's happening it won't be long before you're all out of a job!'

But they didn't hear; they did nothing. Except drink their master's wine, eat his food, and keep taking their wages – plus a bit extra from the provisions allowance. Even if they had heard, short-term greed would have overtaken their long-term view.

Following years of comfortable complaining the estate manager had a smaller estate to look after and the housekeeper and butler had fewer people to manage. To coin a phrase: the end was nigh.

It was a sad day when the government men arrived to assess the value of the estate. They stayed for three days measuring and counting, writing in their big black leather notebooks, talking, pointing and discussing. All the farms were visited and the livestock counted – that which hadn't been hidden – and letters of notice handed out.

When they were about to leave, I had an idea.

'They're taking two carriages and there's only four of them,' I told Trinity. 'There's plenty of space so if we sneak aboard perhaps we can escape across the estate boundary.' I couldn't keep the excitement from my voice.

'We tried something similar some years ago, Albie, remember? In the back of a hand cart.'

'How can I forget. Just our bad luck, the wheel fell off as we reached the last gate.'

'What about that time you tried to float down the stream under the boundary bridge? He, he; every time you got near it you were chased away by angry ducks.'

As the men climbed inside, two to a carriage, Trinity stepped into the leading one and I took the second. Off we trotted. Inside the compartment the men chattered about the condition of the estate. My excitement mounted with every clip-clop of the horses' hooves. I stared from the window at the perimeter hedgerows getting closer. Then we stopped. I heard shouting between the two drivers so stepped down for a look.

Putting my head inside Trinity's door I asked, 'What's happening?'

'I heard the driver say his horse simply stopped and refused to go through the gate.'

I went to see for myself. The driver was tapping his charge on the shoulder with his whip. The old nag was standing still, facing the countryside beyond. When I moved nearer it turned in my direction, neighed gently and nodded its head from side to side as if saying 'No'.

I called Trinity. She floated alongside me as I explained what had happened with the horse. We were standing a few yards from the carriages discussing it when, without warning, the first horse leapt forward and raced through the gateposts followed immediately by the next and they were gone, leaving only muddy wheel ruts and two dispirited spectres in their wake.

'They wouldn't move over the estate border line while we were aboard, would they?'

'No.'

We didn't utter another word as we trudged back to the house.

It was an even sadder day watching the staff leave for the railway station in a couple of carts. We decided not to bother trying to stow away. For Trinity and me the world went strangely silent.

I was pondering the carpet of dust, picturing my dearest Lizzie when I heard a rustle behind me. My brain made the connection and I twisted around expecting to see my fiancée standing there with her beautiful smile. There was someone, and she was smiling. But it wasn't Lizzie. Nor was it Trinity.

'I hope I'm not intruding on your contemplation but . . . are you the famous Albert Hapless?'

Her voice flowed like a tinkling stream; it seemed to sparkle like sunlight on rippling water. Long, silky, blonde hair framed her waif-like face, cascading over narrow shoulders and reaching almost to her slender waist. Her simple shift was the palest of pinks and golds, glowing to match her skin. With her slight body she could be either girl or woman; I couldn't tell.

Some moments later I realised my chin was hanging loose. That was about the time my brain processed her words. *Famous?* I stood up.

'Albert Hapless, yes. Famous, no. You must have the wrong one – although I know of no other, I'm sure. Unless you wanted my granddad, rest his soul, he was an Albert. Died in 1861, I think it was. Who are you? Where'd you come from? I assume you're dead else we wouldn't be talking to each other.' Although she looked too alive to be dead.

'Yes, Albert, I am as dead as you and Trinity. I am Dirroh.' She must have seen my surprise. 'Oh yes, I know about Trinity; you are both famous. She'll be here in a moment. My friend Nettor has gone to find her.' Dirroh's words floated in the air like musical notes.

A duplicate of the strange woman floated through the wall of the drawing room with Trinity, holding hands like two girls at play. Nettor was equally as pretty but with dark-blonde hair ribboned loosely at each side of her head, also reaching to her waist.

She gasped as they stopped beside Dirroh and me. 'Oh! My oh my. Albert. He is so handsome. Wait until the– '

'Nettor!'

Dirroh's voice was a reprimand; Nettor was obviously about to speak out of place.

'These lovely ladies are here to help us, Albie. Nettor told me,' said Trinity.

'How? Help us with what?' I wanted to know. Trinity could be somewhat naïve. 'How do you know our names? How did you get in? Who are you?'

Dirroh had a laugh as light as falling snow. 'So many questions. Let me explain. Can I also call you Albie? Such a sweet name.

'Your names are well-known in the spirit world. Many who have met you have told the story of the innocent ghosts of Ruddyard Park. Condemned to spend your phantom lives imprisoned in these lands,' her voice began to rise, 'unable to haunt the living, frighten children, scare the wits out of people, go where you wish without impediment and have lots and lots of fun. Hahahahahaha!' The laugh didn't have such a prettiness about it.

'It must have been the Armless Army, Albie,' said Trinity. 'Some of them obviously didn't get into Heaven.'

Nettor sniggered at the word. Everyone glared at her.

'Um . . . Armless Army,' she said, 'that's funny.'

Dirroh cut across her. She cleared her throat after the nasty laugh. 'We are called the Glimmers, my friends. As to how we got in, well . . . . Of course, you wouldn't know but normally we spirits can go where we want. Everywhere is open to us. There are no barriers in the spiritsphere. We can go literally anywhere in the world. Doesn't that sound exciting? You see, what happened to you is most unusual; to be bound to one place. It's tragic. You just wait till that Father Brimstone dies; we'll make his life hell. Hahaha!

'I was saying, it's a tragedy. So when we heard about your problem, we said we must go and offer hope to them; help Albert and Trinity to break free.'

'That's what she said,' trilled Nettor.

Trinity was almost bouncing up and down. 'This is so thrilling. How will you get us out, Dirroh? What do we have to do?'

'Now, firstly you have to trust us. Totally. Can you do that?'

'Yes, yes, absolutely,' squealed Trinity. 'We can, can't we Albie? You seem to be such beautiful people. Lovely unusual names too.'

I was more sceptical. Across folded arms I said, 'Dirroh, Nettor, all I want is to clear our names so we can go to Heaven to find our loved ones. As nice as it sounds to be free in the spiritsphere, as you call it, I just want to find my Lizzie. If you can help me do that then I'll do whatever is needed.'

Dirroh smiled and stroked a hand through her hair as she spoke. 'Heaven. Yes, of course. There are ghosts in the outside world who can help with that. Right, Nettor?'

'Everything is possible.'

Dirroh stepped closer to me. She had skin as pure as a baby's. Her voice dropped to a silky whisper. 'It's true, Albie. *Everything* is possible – especially for you.' She stepped away, her voice normal again. 'We don't want you to rush your decision so we will return tomorrow to find out if you can trust us.'

Dirroh and Nettor faded away.

19

'Albie, what's the matter with you? I thought you wanted to escape but you seemed . . . hesitant.'

'I don't want to do all that haunting stuff, Trinity. All I want is to see Lizzie again. Isn't that what you want – to see Daniel again?'

'Yes, yes, of course. But there's no harm in having a bit of fun as well.'

The next day Dirroh materialised while we were in the library; she walked from one of the bookcases.

'You are such handsome ghosts.' Her voice was like honey. 'How are you today?'

Trinity and I had talked for hours the previous night and agreed the Glimmers seemed to be nice spirits; ones we could trust. When we told Dirroh, her smile made the dull room as bright as sunshine.

'How will you get us out? you asked yesterday, Trinity. Let me explain. Before we joined the spiritsphere we Glimmers were, let me say, magicians of a sort. You won't be interested in the detail but, to keep it simple, we can make unusual things happen.'

'And the thing you want to make happen for us is to lift the priest's curse?'

Dirroh caressed Trinity's hair. 'You are so astute for one so young.'

'You and Nettor are also young.'

'Hmn, well, perhaps a few years older than you and Albie. Anyway, I need to know if you are happy for us to use magic on you.'

'I'm not sure I believe in magic,' I said.

'Did you believe in ghosts before you became one?' asked Dirroh with one of her smiles.

I raised my eyebrows. Good point, I thought.

'You must understand I cannot guarantee it will work. The Glimmers can only give you hope.'

'But anything's worth a try, isn't it Albie,' said Trinity.

I nodded silently.

'Because such strong magic is required, we need several Glimmers to concentrate the, er, spell. So, let me introduce some of my friends . . .' several shapes glowed behind her, slowly turning into striking women like Dirroh and Nettor. '. . . Eliv, Detah, Ytrid, Ragluv, Elbirroh and Derrohba.'

Each smiled and waved as their name was given. All had long flowing hair, similar radiant skin and shimmering dresses. If I'm honest, they were the most gorgeous-looking group of young ladies I had ever encountered.

'Wonderful names; so mysterious and ethereal,' purred Trinity.

'Now we must leave you in hope whilst we go and prepare ourselves for the big event. Meet us tomorrow morning at the southern gate. We will be on the outside, beyond your boundary.'

The eight images melted away into the bookcases.

We arrived the next morning as the heavens were transforming from pink to gold ahead of the rising sun. It was March and had rained overnight. The wind was up. The ground was muddy but didn't affect us. The ladies appeared, their iridescence matching that of the joyful sky.

'We have been concentrating all night on the correct enchantment,' Dirroh explained, 'and I need you both to fill yourselves with hope and trust.'

She instructed us to put twenty paces between us and the gate then walk steadily and positively towards her. Of course, Trinity and I had tried this many times in our early days around all the estate margins, but to no avail. We held hands as we strode in the Glimmers' direction. Two paces from the gate my legs became like lead; Trinity was the same. It was exactly as before. Each step felt like withdrawing a boot from the stickiest mud, raising it to chest height before the next one. My foot felt as if it sank back into a quagmire every time. Sucking – tugging – forcing - wrenching – sucking. It was possible to move only a few inches but we persevered. Our movements looked like those of dancing horses.

Both of us had been so intent upon watching our feet we hadn't looked up at the Glimmers. When we did, they had disappeared.

'Dirroh? Nettor?' called Trinity.

The pair came into view. 'We have been watching but faded so we wouldn't distract you. Can you turn around and go back only five paces this time? We must try once more I'm afraid.'

We must have looked like two elephants trying to turn a circle. It took longer to do that than it had taken to stride out in the first place.

It didn't work.

Dirroh was encouraging. 'Albie, give Trinity a piggy-back so she won't get stuck. When you reach the gate, you will be able to launch her over the top bar.'

The rest of the Glimmers came to watch.

That didn't work either. When I got within two yards of the edge I couldn't move.

'Come on Albie, you can do it!' shouted Trinity as if I were a racehorse.

The spectators clapped and cheered.

'Keep going!' shouted Eliv and Ragluv like a pair of twins.

Trinity is as light as a feather but she seemed to be forcing my feet deeper into a swamp.

'I can't! I'm stuck!'

There was a collective sigh from the ladies.

'Shame,' called Detah.

We gave up.

'Try going backwards for the next attempt,' Dirroh suggested. 'It may fool the curse.'

We tried. It didn't.

'Oh Trinity, Albie, we are so sorry,' Dirroh and Nettor had appeared with all the others. Elbirroh has suggested we Glimmers take a rest; the concentration has made them exceptionally tired.' Behind her the young ladies all nodded.

Dirroh joined in. 'You must be weary too. Shall we try once more tomorrow? We need to discuss some new spells. Go and sleep; we'll see you in the morning.'

Trinity and I trudged back to the house, exhausted. We slept most of the day.

On the way back next morning we were full of ideas.

'What if we . . . .'

'Maybe if we tried . . . .'

The Glimmers were waiting, as bright as the morning.

We tried one of my ideas first. As we reached the old gate, I leaned headfirst over the boundary so they could grab my hands and shoulders and pull me across. I heaved my body forward, banged my head into what felt like a brick wall and rebounded onto my back in the field.

Everyone faded away. I was sure I heard invisible muttering. It was ages before the ladies returned.

Trinity's suggestion was similar. She'd noticed the five-bar gate swung out of our field into the next. In her case she climbed onto it so the others could swing it open. When they tried, she bounced back – boing! – but held on as they tried again. Boing! With her arms and legs spread out she looked like a spider that won't let go when you try to shake it off a cloth. I was certain I heard sniggering. Eventually she bounced – boi-oi-oing! – falling flat onto the grass.

'I have an idea,' said Derrohba with an encouraging smile at Trinity. 'Gather around girls.'

The Glimmers formed a circle while she explained they should open the gate as wide as possible so the exit from the field was clear. As they complied, she instructed them to form a line each side like a guard of honour.

'Now Trinity and Albie, you must run as fast as you can at the opening. My theory is your speed will carry you over the threshold and . . . .'

'Yes, yes, yes!' yelled the others like school children at a three-legged race.

Back, back, back we went; fifty or sixty yards. Trinity hitched up her skirts into her drawers. I forgave her behaviour in the circumstances. Then, holding hands, we galloped at the space. The Glimmers cheered, 'Go! Go! You can do it!' In the last few paces, I really believed it was going to work. We slowed, but not as before. We got level with the gateposts . . . .

'Ye-e-e-es!' we screamed together.

Then we hit the invisible wall – boing! – and were suddenly flat on our backs.

As I was shaking my head trying to restore my senses all I heard was raucous, cackling hoots and cries. Trinity and I helped one another to stand. We gawped at the Glimmers. They had collapsed into screeching laughter; leaning on each other's shoulders or rolling on the ground clutching their sides. There were many more of them and some were switching colours from glowing pink and gold to misty grey and black.

I was so angry I shouted, 'What's the matter with you? It's not funny! We're trying to escape this place so we can be with our loved ones! It's not a joke!'

Dirroh appeared in front of us. 'Yes it is, Albie. That's exactly what it is – a joke. And you both looked so hilarious, I can't tell you what fun we've had.' Everyone gathered behind her; the crowd must have numbered about fifty in all. 'It's been one of the best Jesting Journeys we've had in a long time, hasn't it girls?'

'Ye-e-e-e-es!' they screamed.

'But I-I d-don't understand,' mumbled Trinity, close to tears.

'Perhaps if we show you our real selves it might help explain . . . . Girls! Transform!'

Instantly, the world darkened as the brilliant colours disappeared. In front of our eyes Dirroh's beauty melted like a dying flame as she turned into the colour of ashes. Her silken dress became black rags, her slight body hunched beneath a scrawny neck and skeletal head, almost bald but for a few wisps of grey hair. Worst of all was when she spoke. It sounded like a chicken when Mrs Carter was about to wring its neck.

'Allow me to present my little band of merry-makers: The Hag-Ghoulies.' Cackles and cheers filled the air as the other ugly, wizened women waved their arms. 'We are the dead witches of the spiritsphere: the enchanters, sorcerers and the like. We are ghouls, you silly couple, and ghouls are not nice.'

'But you were so n-nice to us, saying you wanted to give us hope. And b-beautiful with such lovely exotic names an-and –' Trinity stuttered.

Dirroh emitted a screech of laughter like a hundred crows escaping hell. 'Oh, you poor stupid child,' she croaked. 'Don't you use your brain? We are the opposite of what we say. You needed a glimmer of hope; we gave you lots of them!

Hahahaha! The Glimmers indeed! And you fell for it.'

Two others joined her; Nettor and Derrohba I think. One spoke. 'You have been voted as the funniest event we have had this year.'

Two voices called from somewhere.

'The piggy-back was my favourite,'

'No, no, swinging Trinity on the gate was the best.'

'What do you mean?' I asked.

The other one replied, 'Usually four times a year we organise a trip for the Haghoulies: a Jesting Journey we call it, to visit other parts of the world to haunt and taunt, and annoy and aggravate, and distract and destroy and do anything we can to get on the whole world's nerves because . . .'

'WE HATE EVERYONE!' the mob screeched amid much crowing.

Suddenly there was total silence. Even the birds stopped singing. Trinity flopped to the ground, leant against the hedge and began to weep. 'There n-never was any h-hope w-was there,' she muttered between sobs. 'When they said the next try might work to free us, they knew it wouldn't because the opposite was true.'

'I've been thinking about that. Take the names but turn them around. Dirroh becomes h-o-r-r-i-d. Nettor becomes r-o-t-t-e-n.'

Trinity picked up a stick and scratched in the dirt – evil, hated, dirty, vulgar, horrible, abhorred.

'These are their real names, Albie.'

'Yes. And they're well-suited to them.' I reached out my hand to help her to her feet. 'Come on, let's go home.'

20

We didn't see the government men again until about forty years later, not long before the Americans arrived. Firstly, came the men in suits wearing small, brimmed hats and shiny black brogues. They checked all the furniture and wrote notes in important-looking leather folders with a gold crown on the front. Next, men in brown coveralls and flat caps arrived; they were the shifters, moving furniture all over the house, wrapping it in old newspapers. That was when we discovered from a discarded paper Britain had been at war with Germany for three years, although for a couple of years we'd suspected something wasn't right in the world beyond Ruddyard Park.

'Look what I've found,' Trinity said rushing from the drawing room one day. 'It's a news sheet: The Daily Mirror, it says July 1942.'

'Hold on,' I pondered for a moment. 'That was about a year ago, wasn't it?'

'I'm not sure; you're the one who keeps track of time. Come on, let's read.'

Trinity and I divided it between us so we could concentrate individually. But we didn't; it was too interesting. We had to share.

'Look, there are articles about British troops fighting battles in north Africa,' I smoothed the sheet and showed Trinity. 'Somewhere in Egypt called El Alamein, there's a map on the front page, against the Panzer Army whatever that is. Do you remember we read all about Egypt and the Pharaohs in one of the books in the library?'

She nodded and carried on reading. 'It says here German ships have destroyed ours, more than twenty of them, in the Arctic Ocean on their way to help the Soviets?' We looked at each other and shrugged. We didn't know who they were or why we should be fighting so far away from home. 'Their battleship named Tirpitz was responsible it says,' Trinity pointed to something else on the page. 'I've got an advertisement here saying women should "make do and mend". What does it mean, do you think?'

'Ha, ha! Nothing you will ever need to worry about Trinity. Mine's got a free cookery book from Stork; something else you won't have to trouble with – and never did!'

She ignored that and continued. 'Even women are fighting. This picture is asking them to join the Women's Land Army. Look, there's a sort of farmworker's uniform.' She pointed to a drawing of one woman sitting on a machine with four big wheels, and another holding a pitchfork. 'Such fun! You didn't smoke, did you, Albie? It's a good thing. Look at this one for cigarettes.'

I gasped. 'Seven pence for ten! I bet not many people smoke them at that price!' I turned a page. 'What are "planes"? It seems American forces borrowed our "planes" to drop bombs in Europe but lost three out of six. Do you know what that means?'

'I think I do now I come to think of it. I hope they've paid for them. The things we've been watching: flying machines as we say,' she pointed vaguely at the ceiling, 'I seem to recall Daniel once referring to them as airy-planes or something similar. Perhaps plane's an abbreviation of that word?'

'So, if I get it, the Americans used flying machines to drop bombs from the sky. That sounds dangerous. People could be hurt.'

'I think that's the idea, Albie.'

It might have been two years earlier Trinity came running to find me in the house one morning and dragged me across the garden into the fields. She pointed into the distance.

'Look, look! In the sky. What do you see?'

It was a beautiful July day I remember. I stared into the summery blue, not a cloud anywhere. No breeze to sway the trees. 'Nothing.'

She pointed again. 'The clump of trees. On the horizon. Just above there.'

'Ah yes, some large birds.' I shielded my eyes with a hand. 'Two? Three? So? We see birds all the time, Trinity.' But I had to admit these looked somehow different. They were flying oddly; straight up or in circles swooping down and up. 'Are they some new breed?'

'Sort of. I spotted them about a week ago and I've been back every day to watch. Sometimes they get closer. Listen. What do you hear?'

I strained my ears trying to cut out the nearby birdsong and buzzing insects. Then I realised.

'I thought it was bees but the sound's too far away. It's a kind of droning. What sort of bird does that, I wonder?'

'Not one we've ever seen. Do you remember many years ago my telling you about Daniel's interest in flying machines? He explained to me how they worked but it was a bit beyond me, I'm afraid.' I had some vague recollection so I nodded. 'I think that's what they are, Albie.'

'Really? But how does it stay up in the sky?'

'That's the bit I couldn't comprehend but I just know it wasn't like Icarus and Daedalus with feathers and wax; it was stronger.'

I butted in. 'Look, look, look, one's coming closer.'

We stared upwards as the giant buzzing bird flew towards us with a noise like a thousand bees. Half way from the horizon it tilted sideways, turned away from us back into the distance until it was barely visible.

I was stunned. 'Why didn't it flap its wings?' I asked Trinity, not expecting an answer.

As is often the case she surprised me. 'I think it's something to do with the air currents?' She curved one hand over the other. 'Like the way the wind blows over its wings; a bird gliding. But I'm not sure.'

On the way back to the house she said, 'They seem only to come out in the early morning so shall we return tomorrow?' She sounded like an excited schoolgirl wanting to catch sight of the boys leaving school.

By the next morning I had it all worked out. I explained to Trinity. 'There must be a man or men on the ground with a long piece of string, like on a kite. They spin it round to get it off the ground then once it's in the sky sort of floating or flying like a kite they can turn it and send it higher or lower. Easy really. Only requires some male logic to work these things out.'

'Hmn,' she hummed. 'I didn't see any string but if there was some it would have to be extraordinarily strong and thick because the flying machine looked quite large and heavy, don't you think? Also, they might need more than one or two men, perhaps?'

It was my turn to 'hmn.'

I stopped; another humming was growing louder and nearer. We searched the sky. Two of the machines were flying in our direction side-by-side, much lower than the one yesterday, only the height of the house. The drone became a scream. It was frightening. We covered our ears.

And they were huge. Far bigger than I'd realised. About the length of two landaus with horses. They had a pointed front with a sort of transparent spinning disc, a long narrow body and wide flat wings. Not really like a bird at all, more a flying crucifix. The noise and the wind were like the breath of a devil. Faster than any steam train I'd ever seen.

Once they'd passed over Trinity shouted, 'Wasn't that exciting? And did you see? On the top? There was a man inside, I'm certain of it!'

'I didn't see anyone. Anyway, it would be impossible for a man to travel at such speed. His heart would be forced from his mouth.'

'Oh! That's disgusting. And stupid. That's what they said about travelling on trains.'

We watched them fly into the distance before they turned and headed back our way. This time they were higher up as they flew one behind the other back to where they started.

After that, we saw them most days but didn't need to go into the fields; they frequently flew over the top of the house, rattling the windows and doors. For a while it was just two of them but as time went by we saw more and more, all painted the same colours: brown and green on top, grey underneath with a red-white-and-blue circle pattern. Sometimes in the night I heard them droning far above my head, sounding like large flocks of machines flying together.

One night Trinity came to my room. 'Albie, something's happening. Come and look.' She took me to a west-facing window on the landing. 'There's a fire somewhere,' she said as we looked out. I could see red reflected in her eyes.

The sky above was black but the skyline was as orange as a summer sunset for miles across. Every now and again the dark horizon flashed yellow. Far distant hollow booms followed.

I frowned as I studied the scene. 'That's more than just a fire,' I said. 'It looks like the whole county is burning.'

We saw the same orangey-red skies on countless nights after that. North, south, east, west;

mostly many, many miles far-off, and always the indistinct ominous rumbling like far-away thunder in a storm.

'Do you think people are burning their own cities to defeat invaders the way Moscow did against Napoleon?'

'We read about that didn't we in one of Sir George's books Lady M left behind. By a Russian soldier who'd been there, do you remember? Very interesting. I suppose it's possible cities are copying the idea. But if they keep doing it at the same rate, there won't be any of Great Britain left. I think there must be a war of some kind happening in those places.'

It was about the same time we discovered something else about our neighbourhood flying machines. They weren't swooping around the heavens for fun. We were in the library trying to find the Atlas of Great Britain which used to be there. We wanted to see which cities might be those that had been alight. Suddenly there was a terrible clattering racket from somewhere above. We rushed outside.

There must have been twenty craft in the sky, more than we'd ever seen at one time. Some had black crosses on their wings unlike the circles we'd been used to seeing. They chased one another, diving towards the fields and climbing into the clouds. At first we thought it was a game until we realised they had some sort of muskets attached to their wings and were shooting. One caught fire; thick black smoke streamed from one of the wings staining the pale blue like spilled ink. Like a taken pheasant it plunged straight to the ground perhaps a mile away where it exploded in a ball of orange flame.

'There's a man in there, Albie,' gasped Trinity. 'We must –'

I felt helpless. 'There's nothing we can do. It's too far away.'

Moments later, a machine leaving a corkscrew of smoke behind wheeled into the ground probably somewhere close to the village.

In total, five of them went the same way before the fight, if that's what it was, broke up. The last one was nearby; it looked as if it had crashed on the estate. We ran at top speed towards the pall of smoke rising from the field. The blazing wreckage lay a hundred yards outside the boundary. The breeze wafted a sweet, smoky smell to us. We couldn't get there. Through the dense cloud a man staggered in our direction, his clothes smouldering. All we could do was watch as he waved and called to us for help.

'He can see us,' said Trinity. 'Over here,' she shouted and beckoned.

A blue-and-yellow fireball filled the sky with debris, scorching the hedge in front of us. And then there was nothing.

'Albie. That poor man. I can't imagine losing Daniel like that. Do you think he had a girlfriend? Or a fiancée? There's no-one here; who will tell her?'

21

Officially, his Post Office title was Boy Messenger but more commonly he was known as the Telegram Boy. Billy was fourteen and delighted he had a 'proper job.' He also had a smart uniform: navy blue with red piping around the cuffs of the jacket and around the collar and edging, and down the seam of the trousers with a matching pill-box hat which he wore at a rakish angle because he thought the girls would notice him. Most importantly, he had a smart, black bike to ride around Oxford in order to deliver his telegrams. Billy enjoyed his work; people were mostly friendly and he liked the fresh air.

But it was wartime. He knew the messages he delivered were only ever one of two types. Unlike the postmen who brought all sorts: friends' letters, keeping in touch letters, news from the front, he only ever delivered good news or bad news. Tonight, the one in his pouch was a bad one.

Although he was on the late shift, it wasn't yet dark. After this he had to go to the fish and chip shop for all the staff back at the office who were also working late. He'd collected the orders for various people's three-penn'orth of chips and would tuck them into his jacket. If the evenings were cold it kept him lovely and warm.

Along with other boys, he'd been watching the dogfights in the distance south and west of the city for the last few days. Many planes had gone

'Here's some more changes. The Prime Minister now is someone called Mr Churchill. It says he has consulted with King George VI over something-or-another to do with a Mr Roosevelt, United States President. It's a different world now, Trinity.'

It was about five years later we waved a sad goodbye to our American friends. For the living ones it was party time; the war was over. They laughed and joked, happy to be going home to loved ones.

We, of course, stayed behind, joining in the doctors' and nurses' fun as best we could. There were still a few patients not yet ready to be moved but fit enough to celebrate. We had become close to several when they were on the verge of death but now their health was improving not all could still see us. We helped as much as we were able by sneaking bottles of beer and the occasional whisky to them. I often wished I could have one.

On the staff, Nurse Closely was our favourite. She was the only one of the medical team able to see and hear us. In the early days of the hospital Trinity came rushing to find me. She was so excited.

'Albie, Albie! I've made a new friend; one of the nurses. I was watching her bandaging a poor man's leg. He was unconscious. Without looking up she said, "What's your name? I'm Nurse Closely. Hilda." I couldn't believe she was talking to me but there was no-one else around so I told her. "Hello

Trinity," she said, "and who's your friend? The man you're usually with?" I told her. She can see us and talk to us, Albie. Isn't it wonderful?'

I agreed. Trinity had arranged to meet the nurse in a quiet corner of what had been the kitchen garden when she stopped working for what she called a "caffeine infusion." She was clutching a cup of coffee in one hand and a cigarette in the other when we arrived.

It was strange to see a woman smoking although I'd noticed one or two of the other nurses did. Smoke drifted from her nostrils as she spoke. 'Hi there Trinity. Hello Albie, I'm Hilda. Pleased to make your acquaintance. So, how long you two been dead? Tell me all about yourselves, why don't you.'

Without being too complicated we tried to explain what had happened together with something of our lives before the fateful night. Hilda listened attentively as she smoked several cigarettes, asking the occasional question. Then we heard someone calling her name from the direction of the house and she excused herself.

'Sorry guys, gotta go, duty calls,' she pronounced it 'dooty'. 'Same time tomorrow?'

We watched her walking away, white dress flapping around her knees. Until then I hadn't noticed she was wearing trousers like the soldiers' uniform but narrower. She straightened her hat, tucking a few stray blonde hairs away.

The next day we discovered how she was able to see and hear us. She was a 'near-death' person.

'When I was sixteen I was a spoilt brat. I'd had my own pony since I was ten. For my birthday my parents gave me a horse. On my first ride we were both nervous. I didn't know his temperament; he didn't understand my controls. Neither of us relaxed. Something spooked him; he threw me. It wasn't his fault but he stomped me.' Hilda paused to light a cigarette from a small silver box with a flame on top. She drew deeply, the end glowed red.

'I was in hospital three years, six months of which I was in a coma. Damaged spine, both legs shattered – hence the pants; trousers to you – fractured skull, broken arms, you name it. Slowly, slowly, the doctors and nurses put me back together again. I was almost twenty when I left the hospital and just past twenty when I went back. Only this time it was to do my medical training. I just knew I wanted to be able to help people the way those guys had helped me. Here I am; thirty, single and glad to be alive.'

Trinity had tears in her eyes; I was close.

After that, we used to meet every now and again when she was off-duty which didn't seem to be often. Twice we helped her play tricks on the doctors and nurses in their 'dormitories' as she called them. In the middle of the night we entered the bedrooms; Trinity in the ladies', me in the men's', and did some noisy moving of various objects including bedcovers. Hilda thought it was hilarious; the rest of the staff didn't.

Ahab and his pals shepherded the less-fortunate ghosts onto various trucks alongside their living colleagues. We all hugged and shook hands before they climbed aboard and were gone with promises to help us if they could. They even took the flag. The place was sad and silent without them. A few days passed and then we said our farewells to Hilda Closely.

Several months later the government shifters returned to load most of the furniture into large pantechnicons; only a few badly-damaged or broken items remained. We stood and watched as our memories of the grand house were taken away by the men in brown coveralls. 1945 was a sad year for us. Trinity and I were truly on our own once more.

I sometimes wondered what had happened to the pieces of furniture. I assumed they'd been sold to pay off some more of Jacob's debts. The day after Trinity had been playing bedroom spy, Arathea joined Rogerson in the sitting room following her walk with Zinnia. Trinity and I followed.

He looked up from his silver attaché case as she entered. They kissed as she sat beside him.

'Doing anything interesting?' she asked, nudging closer.

'Furniture shopping. I'm checking over some of the photos my guys have sent of old Ruddyard Park furniture to buy. Want to look?'

He turned the case towards her so she could see the television part; the light brightened her pale face and reflected in her green eyes. Trinity and I leaned over the back of the settee for a closer look.

'They've found these three Thomas Sheraton chairs; a bit expensive but I think we'll take them. And look at the carving on this George II side table they tracked down in Mexico.'

'Golly, Albie, some of our furniture is in South America.'

Arathea tapped the picture. 'Beautiful. Oh, and this other little table is so pretty. What is it?'

I noticed that today her northern accent was quite strong. I'd become something of an expert when I was there with Lady Margaret. I would say that Arathea was more Cheshire than Lancashire; certainly not from Manchester city or Salford but she probably mixed with those people. Her *oh* didn't sound so much like *orr* and her *other* not like *oother*. Mind you they used to laugh at my accent; or laff as they would say.

'Look, Albie. That table was in my bedroom. Daniel used to say the beauty of the inlaid flowers was surpassed only by the beauty of the lady whose room it was. Me. He meant me'

'I guessed that – not that you spent much time in your own bedroom from what you've told me!'

'Walnut, ebony and ivory marquetry,' Rogerson explained. 'Three hundred and fifty years old. Wow! They found it in a Japanese sale room. The maker's name and date match the government inventory from 1942 when they stripped out a lot of stuff before the Yanks came.'

Our eyes met as they opened wider. 'Japan!'

Trinity reached a hand through Arathea's and pointed at an upholstered chair as she said, 'Do you think Queen Anne really had legs like that, Albie?'

'Hope not, poor woman. I remember that chair. Sir George set light to it one evening when he was roaring drunk. Her ladyship was livid. She came into this room and found him in a cloud of cigar smoke laughing away to himself. I helped the upholsterer load it onto his cart to take for recovering.'

'And now Mr Lovatt is bringing everything back from all over the world: Japan, Mexico. He's a wonderful man, Albie. And handsome too.'

'Enough of that, miss!'

22

Rogerson Lovatt spoke. 'Despite what Kingsley thinks, we've all been well-watered, wined and whiskied, and deliciously-fed by Carla.' He smiled at her. 'Thank you. Now let's get on with the proceedings.'

They held hands around the octagonal table in the drawing room as instructed: Carla – Rogerson – Arathea – Zinnia – Kingsley and back to Carla to complete the circle. A carafe of water and glasses sat on the table between Arathea and Zinnia. The only lighting was from the standard lamps in the corners. The room was dim and as silent as fluff falling from a dusting cloth. The women closed their eyes; the men stared at Carla; her black clothing suitably sombre.

She bowed her head and spoke quietly to the tabletop. 'Spirits of the world, forgive us for disturbing the peace of the peaceful. We wish only to speak to the troubled souls of this house.'

Trinity nudged me. 'That's us,' she said, sitting straighter.

Carla continued. 'All others may return to their restings – unless they have something to tell us.' She looked up at the faces around the table. 'Now, please everyone, we must close eyes and concentrate the ears.'

Kingsley raised his eyebrows at Rogerson but complied.

'I am able to communicate with the dead. Please speak through me or to me as you wish. If you speak through me your words will be for all to hear. If you speak to me, I alone will hear you. I will pass on your message or not, as you wish. Please to tell if you want to be seen by me or anyone else.

'We don't harm you; please don't to harm us. We want to help you so please to help us helping you.'

Trinity stood and walked through everyone to the centre of the table, her legs invisible to me, looking around pausing to stare into each face. 'I want to see if they look serious – especially Nutball. What do you think, Albie?'

I felt agitated and nervous. I didn't know if I wanted to go through with it. As I joined Trinity, Carla gasped. I saw her grasp Rogerson's hand tightly as she swayed her head. She was trembling.

'I think he's trying but we'd better keep an eye on him. What's wrong with Carla?' I asked as we returned to our seats.

Before Trinity could answer, Carla threw back her head and called out, 'Spirits! I hear you. Two people. I feel your presence in this room. Do you wish to show us yourselves? Will you speak to me?'

I grabbed Trinity's hand. 'Argh! She frightened the life out of me!'

'She could hardly do that, Albie.'

'She knows we're here.'

The air tingled like the time she touched an electric-city wire trying to find out how a radio worked. The soldiers had no music for the rest of the day. A pale golden glow surrounded Carla, spreading slowly over the table to the others. She opened her mouth to speak again. Something was happening; I felt drawn to Carla.

'Oh, for Pete's sake! I can't take this crap!' shouted Nutball.

The aura and tingle disappeared. I deflated like a pricked balloon. Trinity and I stared at one another, speechless.

'Oh Kingsley,' said Zinnia,' I was starting to feel something then.'

'Yeah? So was I. I was feeling conned, duped.'

Rogerson said nothing; his eyes spoke for him. If I wasn't already dead and he looked at me like that, I soon would be.

Carla didn't honour him with even a glance. She continued to stare at the ceiling. Her voice was harsh. 'Hold. The. Hands. EVERYONE!'

Trinity and I stared at each other in surprise. Unexpectedly, Carla did not sound like someone to be trifled with.

There was an embarrassed shuffling. Zinnia grasped Kingsley as she rasped something in his ear. Reluctantly he took Carla's palm in his.

'Spirits, we are nervous. I am sorry for this. If you can make a sign to us . . . to prove your presence?'

I nudged Trinity and whispered, 'Harpsichord.'

'I'd rather tip that carafe of water over him.'

'Ha, ha, so would I but I don't think it would help our cause. Tell you what; you play the harpsichord and I'll do something less dangerous with the water.'

There were nervous murmurs whilst Trinity tinkled on the keys. Kingsley was about to speak when I slid one of the glasses across the tabletop to rest in front of him.

'OK, who's doing the trick?' he asked. 'Come on, own—'

'Oh my God!' Arathea exclaimed.

Kingsley seemed to have lost the power of speech as I raised the carafe high, circling above their heads before lowering it to the glass. I poured some water and returned the carafe. Trinity joined me, a huge smile on her face. She nodded at Carla. I looked over to see the corners of her mouth turned up at our little display.

'Spirits we thank you.' She threw back her head once more. 'We want to help. Please speak to me or through me.' Her glow was returning. 'Will you speak to us now. We are *all* listening this time.' The aura spread slowly over the group, including the sceptical one.

'Go on, you go,' said Trinity.

'No, you're better with words than me.'

'Than *I* not *me*.'

'See what I mean.'

'You're the man.'

'But I'm only a footman.'

'In that case I command you to go! Go on, they're waiting.'

Then I heard Carla's voice in my head but her lips weren't moving. It was obvious from Trinity's face she was experiencing the same thing.

'Please do not be frightened of me. I am a friend. Start by thinking of your name.'

I stared at Carla's closed eyes and said to myself: Albert.

The voice continued in my head. *'Hello Albert. Hello Trinity. Can I tell the others your names?'*

I gripped Trinity's hand as we looked at each other, nodding busily.

'Yes.' I thought. Trinity must have done the same.

'Everyone, I am in communication with Albert and Trinity.' Four pairs of eyes sprung open upon hearing Carla's words.

Arathea spoke across the table. 'Trinity? Wasn't that name mentioned in Kingsley's history book?'

'Yes,' said Zinnia, then turned to Nutball, 'she was Washbury's fiancée, wasn't she?'

'Described as the notorious . . . no, rebellious, Miss Trinity Hope, I believe,' offered Kingsley.

Carla shushed them then spoke to our minds somehow. *'Spirit? Are you that Trinity?'*

I heard Trinity respond. *'Yes.'*

'And Albert, what is your name?'

'Albert Hapless, footman. But everyone calls me Albie, Miss Carla.'

'Everyone. We are joined by Trinity Hope and Albert, or Albie, Hapless, footman.'

I saw Nutball was about to speak; probably something about traitors but Carla cut him off with a glare.

'Albie? Trinity? Would you like everyone to hear you from your own lips or through mine?'

'What do you think, Albie?' asked Trinity.

'I think everyone should hear our story – especially Shadwick Nutball – from us, don't you?'

'Agreed.'

'Miss Carla, we'd like to be able to tell everyone our story ourselves if that's alright with you. Trinity wants me to do the talking but don't think for a moment that will stop her joining in or contradicting me or correcting my grammar.'

Carla smiled as she addressed the table. 'Friends. Albie and Trinity would speak to us all so in a moment you will hear their voices but you won't to see them. Do not stop with the hands. Spirits, speak up. Please introduce yourselves.'

Trinity nudged me to go first. 'Good evening. Um. My name is Albie . . . .' My voice sounded strange, like an echo.

'You sound like the voices on the radio, Albie. How odd,' whispered Trinity. 'Carry on.'

I was told once if you speak louder you don't sound as nervous, so I tried. 'I'm Albie Hapless and I was a footman in the employ of Mr Daniel Washbury in this household. Before that I was footman to Sir George and Lady Margaret Kingswood, also in this house. I was born on the Ruddyard Park estate in the Year of Our Lord 1849 and joined the household in 1859.'

'And I am Trinity Hope, born in Derbyshire in 1851. I was Daniel Washbury's fiancée until . . . .' Trinity started to snivel.

'Sorry. She's feeling emotional. We both do when we think about our loved ones: her Daniel and my Lizzie.'

'Thank you both. I think you know our names already, yes?' Carla smiled in our direction. 'You have been with us all the time, no?'

'Er, yes, no,' I replied, a bit confused over the way she put things. 'And we'd like to tell the angry Doctor, excuse me, ghosts do exist as he can see. Well, not see but hear.' Everyone laughed which helped me relax a little. 'And we'd like to thank Mr Lovatt for bringing the house back to life. What you are doing, sir, is wonderful.'

'Beautiful,' added Trinity, still sounding sniffy.

Rogerson smiled and said, 'Thank you, Trinity and Albie. We know a little of your story and feel sorry for you so what can we do to help?'

Nutball began to speak; his words surprised me. 'Thank you for putting me in my place, Albie. Why don't you tell us what happened on the night you, erm, passed.'

Trinity replied sharply. 'It's alright to say *died* or *were killed*; we've had a hundred-and-forty or more years to get used to the idea.'

'Don't be rude, Trinity,' I said. I was reminded everyone could hear us by their sniggers. I continued, 'They're going to help us. Sorry Mr Shadwick, she's just a bit . . . tense.'

'It's OK, Albie. That's interesting though; you called me Shadwick. Why was that?'

'As soon as you arrived, we said you reminded us of the butler who was serving here at the time: Jeremiah Shadwick. Your features are the same. Then we heard you say you were related to him and . . . a slip of the tongue. No offence, sir,' I said trying to be as polite as possible even though I still didn't trust him. I could swallow my pride along with the best of them.

'So. You are troubled,' said Carla, 'that is why you are here still. You cannot full escape this life. Tell us what's happen on the day you died. We all work together to remove your problems.'

Trying not to gabble, Trinity and I explained everything: Daniel, Lizzie, the plotters, the railways, the police, and finally the shooting. The group remained silent like school children listening to a teacher telling a story. It took us more than an hour. And Trinity didn't once correct my grammar. When we finished they looked stunned, rigid on their chairs, staring in our direction.

'Amazing.'

'Fascinating.'

'Wow.'

'Most interesting.'

'We thank you for living again with your . . . trauma? That is correct word?'

'Precisely the correct word, Carla,' confirmed Trinity.

Carla smiled. 'Do you both mind if we take a little break. I can see Dr Nutball needs a drink and

I think the ladies may want to freshen up. You will wait for us?'

We acknowledged her and sat chatting after they left the room.

'What do you think?' I asked.

'Albie, I'm so excited. We're talking to live people for the first time in our . . . deaths. It's like a dream come true. They're listening to us; people who can help us to set the record straight, tell the world the truth.'

'But they have to be able to prove it and for that we need Lady M's letter.'

'And we don't know where Daniel hid it.'

Our audience returned, taking the same places at the table. Carla asked if we were still in the room which we confirmed. She told the others they no longer needed to hold hands but I saw Zinnia grab Kingsley's and Arathea took Rogerson's in hers.

Rogerson spoke first. 'Albie, you told us you had some papers incriminating Shadwick. Is it possible to see them?'

'Do you know where they are?' asked Trinity.

'Still in Shadwick's old room under the floor I suppose.'

'You suppose! Haven't you checked?'

'Yes of course . . . but not for a while.'

'When exactly?'

'I don't know; time goes so slowly. Not since the Americans left, anyway.'

'That was seventy years ago! Go and look this instant!'

I smiled at the group who were staring at us but, of course, they couldn't see. I hate it when Trinity gets mad with me so I scampered through the wall taking the shortest route to the back stairs. The sound of laughter followed me.

I hadn't been in the room for a long, long time. I imagined when it was Shadwick's and pictured him lying here at the end of the day, feeling smug. Thinking himself clever he'd tricked his way into the house and job. Self-satisfied he'd betrayed Mr Daniel for a reason only he knew. Scheming to get his hands on my Lizzie. Thinking of him made my blood boil so much I wanted to go back downstairs and bash Nutball on the nose for looking like him.

Mousey didn't seem to be around. I pulled up the loose corner board and felt inside. Nothing. I wished I'd brought a candle with me; it was as black as the old coal cellar. I didn't know if the electric-city worked in the servants' quarters but I felt around the wall towards the door, found the switch and flicked it. A buzz and crackle above my head then the room glowed with light. The bed had gone but the metal bed ends leaned against the wall beneath the window. I checked the hole once more. Nothing. I managed to remove the adjacent floorboards. Still nothing. Our big chance and I'd messed it up. I dragged my feet towards the door dreading telling everyone how useless I was. Trinity would kill me – if I wasn't already dead!

23

I turned off the light, paused then immediately switched it back on. No, I wasn't mistaken.

Scratch, scratch.

I looked down. Black nose, twitching whiskers, shiny eyes.

'Mousey! My little friend – probably my only friend now. How are you?'

He ran up my hose and back again looking as excited as a mouse who'd stolen cheese from a trap. Then he scurried to the empty hole. I stepped over to him but he was gone.

Scratch, scratch.

I turned around but he was nowhere to be seen. On my hands and knees, I followed the sound. It was coming from further along the floor. Suddenly a tiny nose popped out of a small knot hole the size of my little finger then disappeared. Next he was running over my hand to the hole and back just like he did when we first met. I knew he was telling me to lift the long board with my finger. So I did. What I saw took me by surprise.

'Mousey! What have we here?'

Eight eyes like black beads stared up at me. Three baby mice and an adult nestled into a bed. A bed made from a cloth pocket with a mattress of yellowed papers. Mousey jumped into the hole and ran over and over the makeshift quilt until Mrs Mousey and the children got up.

'You got married and . . . I didn't know ghosts could have children or even have . . . you know. Congratulations!' I reached down and lifted the pocket out. 'You just saved my life – in a manner of speaking.'

He seemed to be explaining to the family what was happening. Mrs Mousey looked sad-eyed; the children's whiskers no longer twitched but drooped. I only needed the papers so returned their cloth bed. Mr and Mrs Mousey and the little ones immediately snuggled inside the pocket. I replaced the roof to their little house and switched off the light.

'Good night, sleep tight.'

As I walked through the wall of the drawing room Trinity was speaking, Arathea was giggling.

'. . . and so glad you can't see what I'm wearing. It was once a beautiful gold satin gown but when the wall fell onto Albie and me it was ripped and some of the lace was torn off. As for my hose . . . . Ah, the intrepid explorer returns.'

They gawped in my direction, faces full of awe. I realised all they could see was a sheaf of papers floating across the room.

'My apologies for the delay; I ran into an old friend and had to meet the family.'

'You mean there are other ghosts here?' asked Arathea.

'Er, no. Just a little joke of ours,' I said, placing my treasure on the table in front of Carla. Even after all these years, it felt strange not presenting the documents on a silver tray.

'May I see?' asked Kingsley, reaching for the papers. 'Shadwick was my relation after all.'

Carla allowed him to take them. I was pleased to see him handling them delicately as he unfolded the sheets. After reading, he slid each one along the table for the others to see, eventually ending back with Carla. While they were doing that Trinity whispered to me.

'Why were you such a long time?'

'My little mouse friend had moved them into his new home. It's only next door but much more spacious, which he needs now he has a family.'

'Family? You mean children?' I nodded. 'I didn't know ghosts could . . . .'

'That's what I said to him.'

'What did he say?'

'He said he never discusses his personal life.' I paused. 'He's a mouse, Trinity; he can't speak, silly!'

Carla broke the silence. 'I think we can all see why he is suspect. Rogerson will keep this safe for you. But it is not enough.'

'If only you could talk to Daniel or Lizzie,' Trinity sounded dejected.

I added, 'They're the only ones who know what happened to Lady Margaret's letter after it was handed over.'

'Is that possible, Carla?' asked Zinnia. 'Where are they? I mean where did they die? Kingsley?'

'As far as I know . . .' a wave of compassion seemed to pass over him as he gazed towards

Trinity's voice. '. . . they . . . died in prison. The history book we read isn't clear on that point.'

Without warning, Carla got to her feet, fingers massaging her temples. 'I'm not sure, Zinnia. Maybe. Maybe. I need to be alone. Ten minutes. Excuse me.' She walked abruptly from the room.

'Perhaps she needs to do some sort of spiritual meditation,' suggested Rogerson, tapping the table. 'We should stay.'

'Or she just needs the loo,' added Kingsley.

He stood away from the table.

'Where are you going, Kingsley?' asked Rogerson, frowning.

'Nowhere, don't worry. Just stretching my legs.'

Rogerson also stood, almost in readiness to prevent Nutball should he try to escape.

'It's warm in here,' he said as he rolled up the long sleeves on his shirt. His forearms were as thick as a master baker's.

'Albie,' said Zinnia, fluffing out her chiffons,' we were asking Trinity what she looked like and what she was wearing. She said she was tall and slim like Arathea.'

'Did she? No, she's short and stout with a big—'

'Ha ha. That's what she said about you.'

'Oh, did she, indeed,' I said over Trinity's fit of the sniggers.

'Actually, as a footman it was customary to be above average height because in the old days the job was to provide protection to the employers when they were out in their carriage.'

'I remember reading about that somewhere,' said Rogerson. 'Didn't the employers try to hire footmen of matching size so they looked better together.'

'Like bookends?' said Zinnia sounding shocked. 'I don't believe that.'

I smiled. 'I suppose our old ways seem strange to you. In the wealthy households that sort of thing did happen but that was before my time. Last time Mrs Carter; she was our cook, measured me I was two inches below the top of the kitchen door which she said was six feet high.'

'Sorry, I was only teasing earlier,' Trinity told them. 'Albie is quite tall; about the same as you, Mr Lovatt, and fairly strong but I'm not quite as tall as I said; a bit less than Arathea.'

Arathea sat up straighter in her chair as she listened.

'Did you wear a uniform?' asked Zinnia.

I described for everybody the uniforms traditionally worn by first and second footmen and others in the household such as the maids like Lizzie.

'So, are you still wearing yours now?' said Arathea.

'What's left of it Miss Arathea. I'm glad you can't see us; we look . . . a little untidy.'

Trinity tried tucking behind her ear a long wave of black hair which had been wayward for the last hundred-and-fifty-years. It fell back again.

Almost as if she'd floated in like another phantom, Carla was back in her seat at the table.

'The house remembers Daniel Washbury.'

'You've been talking to the house?' Kingsley sounded disbelieving as he sat.

'In a way you would not understand. Trinity, we must act the play of the night you died. I must stand where you saw your fiancé standing; I must see the things you didn't see in the room.' Carla stood. 'Guide me please. Is room same as it was? Furniture in same places?'

It took a moment or two for Trinity to catch on. In fact, everyone looked confused.

'Yes, yes, I think so. I understand. Er, I must look at the room from outside the door. Wait.' Trinity tried the door but found it too heavy. 'Normally we don't bother opening doors. Mr Lovatt, I wonder if you could oblige, please?' Once the door was open, Trinity glided into the hall then called back. 'Walk towards the fireplace.'

Carla followed directions until Trinity was satisfied Carla was standing in Daniel's position. Next she asked who else could be seen and where they were standing. We all watched in fascination as Carla moved about the room to stand near the doorway where Lizzie had been. Then she stood at the door first before stepping a little way into the room representing the positions of the two plotters. Finally, she returned to Daniel's place by the mantlepiece where Trinity said he'd been brandishing his ceremonial sword.

Carla spoke to everyone. 'Next what you see and hear will be strange . . . '

'As if it's not strange enough already,' quipped Kingsley.

'. . . but you must be total quiet. With the help of the house I am to become Daniel Washbury on that night. I will move in a funny way and speak in a different voice. Especially for Kingsley: do not mock. What I do is extremely hard.' She closed her eyes. 'Now I begin.'

Carla stood like a rock and took several deep breaths. She swayed, everyone gasped. She grabbed the mantlepiece to steady herself. Suddenly her eyes were large and staring like the old mad woman who used to chase the kids in the village. She looked at the doorway.

The voice that came from her body was from deep down in her belly, rumbling at the back of her throat. It was Carla but not the voice we knew.

'Leave her Oddfellow! She's only a maid. Leave her alone, I say!'

She paused as if listening to someone.

Trinity whispered to me, her voice shaking, 'Oh Albie, it's Daniel! She's speaking Daniel's words.' There were tears in her eyes.

'Don't hurt her, she's not a spy you damned fool. Lizzie, I'm sorry for this. Anyway, I want no part in your insane adventure. Tell him, Bristler.'

More listening.

'Give me the letter, sir. She says it's private.' Carla held out her hand. 'For God's sake man! Yes, I will keep it safe but I am certain it has nothing to do with your scatter-brained proposal.

Leave her alone! Her screaming will wake the servants.'

'What about Shadwick? How would you know if he's awake or not?' Pause. 'Oh, that's how you got in. I shall have words with him in the morning.'

Carla reached above the fireplace for the sword, removed it from the scabbard and waved it in the direction of the door.

'Kicking the door won't help, man. You're a brute, Oddfellow! Bristler, help the child into a chair. Do that again Oddfellow and you will have me to answer to.' Carla pointed the sword. 'I'm sorry, Lizzie. Yes, I have the letter, dear. Look, I'm putting it somewhere safe to read later.'

Carla began struggling with the sword handle, twisting and turning it. She waved it at the doorway.

'Now, get out of my house! You will not use my property for storing explosives. I want no part of your plan. In the morning I intend to inform the authorities of your anarchy and advise my neighbour Outlandish that his life is in danger. So, leave—' Pause. 'What was that noise? Who . . . ?' She laid the sword on the shelf. 'In God's name, what's happening?'

Carla put her hands to her head and sunk slowly to the floor holding onto the chair where the scabbard was resting. Everyone rushed over to her, including Trinity and me, even though we couldn't help. Kingsley put his fingers against the side of her neck.

'She's fainted. Lay her down here. Cushion somebody?' Arathea grabbed one from the other fireside chair. Kingsley set it behind Carla's head as they laid her flat.

'Should I fetch some brandy?' asked Zinnia.

'I could do with one,' said Arathea. 'Oh, for Carla you mean.'

'No brandy,' said Kingsley. 'That's only in the movies.' I vaguely recalled the Americans using that word but couldn't remember what it meant. I mouthed 'movies ?' as I looked at Trinity but she only shrugged. 'Fruit juice is better than alcohol. Pull that chair here please Rogerson so we can raise her legs. She'll be OK in a couple of minutes if we give her some air.'

I said to Trinity, 'Mrs Carter used to keep a tiny phial of ammonia and rosemary for these situations. One sniff of that'd have you awake in no time.'

Everyone moved away but stood staring at Carla. Zinnia moved closer to Kingsley, surreptitiously taking his hand. I nudged Trinity and nodded my head so she would see.

'I loved the way you took charge. So masterful,' Zinnia whispered.

'Darling, that was so weird,' Arathea said to Rogerson. He said something I didn't hear and she left the room.

'I think, Albie,' said Trinity quietly, her eyes wet, 'that was one of the strangest experiences of my life, er . . . death . . . or both. She was speaking Daniel's words; it was as if he were here.'

'He tried to protect Lizzie. Did you hear?'

'Yes, that was exactly what Daniel would do but I didn't understand what Carla was doing with the letter and the sword, did you?'

'No. Maybe we can ask her; she's regaining her senses, look.'

Kingsley helped Carla sit upright and instructed her to put her head between her knees for a minute before helping her to her feet and asking how she felt. I noticed he was very attentive and gentle with her and began to change my mind about him. Trinity seemed to feel the same.

'Perhaps he's a real doctor after all,' she said. Then she whispered, 'Or maybe he's taken a shine to Miss Carla?'

The group reconvened at the octagonal table just as Arathea came through the door bearing a tray with a decanter, five brandy goblets and a glass of orange juice. She looked far too tall to be a maid. She poured four brandies and checked with Carla.

'Kingsley said you should have orange juice. What would—?'

'Kingsley is wrong then. Please to pour me a brandy, Arathea.'

'Large or small?'

Kingsley laughed. 'Got to be a *medium*, hasn't it?'

Carla smiled. 'Very good joke, Doctor. You are becoming more normal person.'

'Thank you for the compliment, Carla. Do you want to tell us what happened?'

'It is difficult. Trinity? Albie? You are still with us?' We confirmed we were. 'So, to try to explain. Buildings remember things. Please don't ask me how; I don't know, but I learn this from my grandmother. I think they don't know everything but they remember big events when there is plenty emotion in the air; things like birth, death, arguments. Serious things. From how Trinity described I believed the house would know that evening. It did. So, I must become part of the house and its memories; I absorb this and become part of it. In other words, I become Daniel Washbury. I live what he lived. He was fine man.'

'Yes, he was,' said Trinity. 'He wanted nothing to do with those terrible men; he didn't even know they were coming.'

'That's right,' I added. 'What we all saw proved that Shadwick was in on it somewhere just like I suspected from those papers.'

'I guess I should apologise for my ancestor,' said Kingsley. 'More brandy, Carla?'

'Oh, sorry, I didn't mean to drink so quick. The re-living experience is very tiring. But to answer Albie and Trinity's problem we need the sword.'

In a flash I leapt to the fireplace, grabbed the weapon and scabbard and laid them on the table. There were gasps as they watched them floating across the room.

'I don't think I'll ever get used to seeing things drifting around in mid-air,' said Arathea. 'So, this isn't a real sword?'

Rogerson replied. 'Only in the sense it wasn't made for fighting anyone; it's a ceremonial one, hence the ornate tassels. People don't do it often nowadays but it was awarded, like a medal, to an individual to commemorate a special action or service provided. In this case to Daniel Washbury for services to the railways.'

Arathea seemed fascinated. She lifted it, weighing it in her hands before handing it to Carla.

'The reason I . . . he had the sword wasn't to threaten men but hide the letter. The handle is hollow and should unscrew but, it is old and I am not strong, I couldn't undo it.'

'Trinity, all those times I searched the room, I never thought of that. A secret compartment. Very clever.'

She grasped my hand. 'This is so exciting. We're going to see the letter.'

24

'No, I can't shift it either,' said Kingsley as he strained to twist the handle.

We'd already watched Rogerson having a go; he was much stronger than the doctor. I could see Trinity admiring his flexing arm muscles. They'd tried rotating it left and right, pushing or pulling and turning at the same time, looking for hidden buttons or catches to release it but nothing worked.

I was almost in tears. Trinity put her arm around my shoulder, hair brushing across my cheek.

'Don't fret, Albie, there must be a way. Carla, in your trance did the handle actually come off?'

'Yes. Daniel held it as Kingsley now does . . .' she closed her eyes for a few moments as she spoke, moving her hands in front of her, 'turned the handle like this, towards me. I had it in my right hand with the blade in my left. He put the letter inside.'

'But that was in your head. We didn't see it come apart. Did anybody?' No-one answered.

Zinnia took the sword from Kingsley, holding it by the blade as she shook her flowing sleeves out of the way. 'I didn't realise it wasn't sharp but it didn't need to be I suppose,' she said, turning and admiring the engraving on the gleaming steel. The reflected light flashed across everyone's eyes. 'Beautifully made.'

Arathea leaned forward. 'Auntie, hold it still . . . just there. Rogerson?' Arathea pointed at the blade closest to the hilt. 'Is that . . . .'

'What is it? What's the matter?' I asked, urgently.

Rogerson answered slowly. 'It's the manufacturer's name and date, Albie. It was made in 1998.'

I leapt forward. 'No, no, no,' I cried, 'It was made in 1860-something or other, wasn't it Trinity?'

'It's not the original?' said Kingsley, taking the sword from Zinnia to check the inscription.

'But it must be. It has to be! We recognise it, don't we Trinity? If it's not, where *is* the original?' I demanded. I felt like I was going mad. 'Carla, you must find out! Please!'

'I don't know where it is,' said Rogerson, 'but hold on a minute.'

In his hand he had the black block I'd heard him call a tablet like a miniature television. He began tapping it with his fingers.

I sat with my head in my hands, Trinity's arm still around my shoulder like a consoling mother. She patted my back. My eyes filled with the tears of years of frustration.

Trinity spoke quietly and gently to me. 'Don't worry Albie, these are all good people who are trying to help us. And they're live people so they can get things done. It will be alright.'

'OK, I've got the inventory,' said Rogerson, sliding a finger across his tablet. I walked through the table for a better look at what he was reading. 'Here we are.' He looked at where I'd been sitting.

'I'm here,' I said, 'next to you.'

I read the description.

Based on the 1822 Light Cavalry pattern, the sword is slightly curved and spear-pointed. It is made of carbon steel, length 34 inches. The hilt is the half-basket style with three fluted bars. Blade width at the hilt is 1 inch.

The grip is black fish-skin bound with silver-plated copper wire. The pommel is a stepped design.

The scabbard is nickel-plated steel with rings.

Sword knots are full dress versions of gold and silver cords and tassels.

'There's a note from my team leader saying they were unable to buy the original – not for sale, apparently – but managed to track down this replica to a specialist in London. Those were their instructions from me: if the original is unavailable, buy a replica. If that's not available check with me about commissioning one.'

'So where's the real one?' asked Kingsley.

Rogerson's fingers were tapping and sliding all over the face of the tablet. Words and pictures flashed by faster than I could read them. I beckoned Trinity over to see. She must have been in one of her polite moods; she walked around the table instead of through it, holding the skirt of her dress as if worried she might knock something. I watched as she passed everyone. Carla drew in her breath as Trinity crossed behind her.

'Trinity? Have you moved? Are you near? I can feel you.'

'I'm standing behind you.'

With Trinity's voice almost next to him Rogerson stopped what he was doing to stare at Carla.

Carla twisted in her chair, looked up, mumbled something and fainted, falling sideways into Kingsley's lap. He tapped her cheek several times. Arathea reached across the table and poured more brandy into Carla's glass. Kingsley took no notice. Carla opened her eyes, looking surprised to find herself in Kingsley's arms.

'Let me help you up,' said Zinnia, a little sharply as she stood, a flash of colour, and pushed Carla's head and shoulders away from Kingsley's encircling hold. 'What happened?'

Carla's voice trembled. 'I-I saw . . . I can see . . . I see you Trinity. You are beautiful.'

'Oh Carla.' Trinity leaned down to embrace Carla but her arms crossed right through her. 'H-how? Can you see Albie too?'

Carla shivered. 'Only you.'

I glanced down at my tattered, once-blue uniform and buckle-less shoe, glad they couldn't see me. I looked disgraceful.

Everyone was frozen in place gawking at the air from where Trinity's voice spoke to Carla. Arathea still held the decanter, Zinnia was half-way to sitting back down, Rogerson's hand hovered over his tablet and Kingsley's arms were open as if continuing to embrace Carla.

The two women asked what Trinity looked like. Carla either didn't hear or ignored them. She addressed Trinity.

Carla spoke slowly and carefully. 'I think perhaps it is because I might have some of the sharing of your fiancé's spirit mixed with my own. Some of his memories maybe stay with me. Because he loved you so much . . . I-I can see you as if I were him.'

Trinity, Arathea and Zinnia burst into tears. So did I.

'Sorry Trinity, I didn't mean to upset you.'

'I'm . . . I'm not upset, I'm happy . . . s-so happy Daniel loves me,' said Trinity, smiling and wiping her eyes. 'I miss him so much.'

'Aaah,' cooed Arathea and Zinnia each reaching for the other's hand.

Carla smiled back at her. 'Then we must see what we do to get you to him again. Rogerson?'

'Hmn? Oh yes, the sword, here it is. Ha, ha, it sounds like somewhere you should know about, Kingsley. It's in a place called BAAMY: the British Armour and Arms Museum of Yesteryear.'

'Let me see,' Kingsley reached for the tablet. 'You're right actually, I do know this place; I passed it on the way here, about twenty miles back.' He tapped the tablet and a coloured map appeared like magic. 'There you are, just down the road. It's a historic listed building like this one.' Kingsley jumped to his feet. 'Right! Give me the sword! Where's the rest of it?'

I slid the scabbard across the table. Nobody reacted; they were getting used to ghostly goings-on.

'What are you going to do?' I asked, excited by his sudden drive.

'I'm going there to get your letter, Albie.' He straightened his glasses. 'Immediately!'

'Oh Kingsley, you're so chivalrous,' fawned Zinnia.

Carla chuckled as she swirled the brandy in her goblet before taking a sip.

'I'll come with you,' Rogerson volunteered.

'And me,' said Arathea.

'And me,' I added before realising it was impossible.

'No, no, this is something I would like to do on my own – to atone for my disgraceful ancestor, Shadwick. But for him, Albie and Trinity would be with their loved ones now – and would have been for a long, long time.'

He held the sword in front of him looking every inch like the drawing of Ivanhoe in the Walter Scott book we had in the library. He stood, ready to go into battle to fight for King and country.

Zinnia fawned some more. 'So brave. But how will you get in? It's late, they'll be closed.

'Leave it to me,' he said striding to the door. 'I'll be back within an hour,' he called over his shoulder as he disappeared into the hall. I could almost hear his armour clanking as he went.

We all stared after him, speechless, until we heard the front door slam, then everyone spoke at once.

'What's got into him?'

'Not like Kingsley at all.'

'So gallant.'

'He is more brave than I expected. Maybe I misjudge him.'

'More brandy anyone?'

Trinity pulled me to one side as Zinnia reached for the decanter. 'Albie, shall we go with him?'

'We can't Trinity, it's off the estate. You know what happens if we try to leave.'

'Oh, yes. But it's so exhilarating – Carla seeing me and all the action. I feel something is going to happen for us tonight.'

Trinity jumped up and down, hugging me. Whilst the ladies chattered away, Rogerson kept tapping his tablet. Eventually Arathea asked what he was doing.

'Tracking him from his phone's satnav.'

Trinity and I looked at each other in bewilderment at Rogerson's strange language. We returned to the table to watch what he was doing. He was pointing at a tiny dot moving across the map, telling the others it was Kingsley.

'Wow, he's almost there,' said Arathea. 'He must be driving fast. He really has got the bit between his teeth, hasn't he.'

While all this was happening, Carla had left the room. She now returned with a coffee tray, cups jingling as she crossed the room. I wanted to help her; it seemed strange: me, downstairs staff, watching an upstairs person carrying a tray. Carla's position was an odd one anyway. Rogerson called her the housekeeper but treated her as an equal. I supposed that's how things were done in the twenty-first century.

'I thought perhaps we need something to keep us all awake – and not getting too drunk. Everyone?'

'Yes please,' they answered together.

While she was pouring, I went to speak to her. 'Miss Carla, we are so grateful to you, and the others of course, for helping Trinity and me. We've met lots of other people, well ghosts really, who have said they would help if they could – and I'm sure they tried – but Dr Nutball dashing off like that for us it's, it's . . . just so kind. We feel so lucky you and your friends came to stay.'

'Thank you, Albie. It is my, our, pleasure. I also know what it is like to—'

'He's there! He's stopped!' squealed Arathea.

Everyone clustered around Rogerson for a few moments watching nothing happening on the tablet. Carla gave them a minute or so before passing around the coffee cups. They sipped. Zinnia screamed, almost dropping her cup as Rogerson's jacket began playing a tune. He pulled his electric-city telephone from his pocket.

'It's Kingsley,' he told everyone. 'I'll put you on speaker.' He laid the instrument on the table from where it started speaking.

'They won't let me in. I explained it to the security chap but he wasn't interested. Patronising fool told me I must be drunk with such a story and that I stunk of alcohol. Damned cheek! When I told him I was a psychiatrist he said: In that case, sir, you ought to know better!'

Rogerson answered, 'Best come on back. We'll sleep on it and see what can be done in the morning.'

'Not likely. I have a Plan B.'

'What Plan B is that, Kingsley?'

'I'm going to break in and steal the sword. See you in about half-an-hour.'

'Kingsley! King—? He's gone.'

There was absolute silence. Zinnia had her hand to her mouth, rainbow nails against her white face. Arathea stared at Carla who was looking at the telephone. Trinity drifted over to the other side of the harpsichord then signalled me to follow.

'I'm not sure this is the best time for a tune Trinity.'

'Oh dear. Do you think we've done the wrong thing, Albie?' she whispered, so low I could barely hear. 'I mean, what if he gets caught?'

'It's not really our fault, is it? We didn't ask him to do anything illegal, did we?'

'That's true, but he's doing it for us. Doesn't that make us culpable?'

'What's that mean?'

'Responsible.'

'Hmn, see what you mean. Look at them, they all look so worried now. Maybe I was wrong about the music. Why don't you play some nice, jolly music to cheer them up, eh?' She agreed so I announced in my best Master of Ceremonies voice, 'Ladies and Sir, for your henjoyment, gratification and hall-round hamusement may I present the hextensive talents of Miss Trinity 'ope a-tinkling on the 'arpsichord. Thank you.'

Everyone laughed, searching for the source of the speech. As Trinity began, the laughter turned to applause before they sat back at the table to listen. She managed to play three bright airs, being congratulated on each as she finished. Just as she played the opening chords of a fourth, another tune interrupted: Rogerson's telephone.

'It's me,' Kingsley's breathless voice called out from the tabletop. 'I've got it! There's a problem!' Before Rogerson could ask what it was, we were told, 'They called the police! I'm being chased!' he puffed. 'See you in fifteen!'

This time it was Zinnia's turn to faint and Carla's to play doctor by gently tapping her cheek.

'I don't know about you Albie but I wish I could have one of those brandies,' Trinity said, grabbing my hand.

'I'm inclined to agree with you. Do you think they'll have any brandy, you know, up there where we'll be going?'

'At this moment, Albie, I wouldn't like to place a wager on which direction we'll be off to after all this.'

Zinnia came around wanting to know what should be done to help Kingsley if the police turned up. No-one had any immediate suggestions. After a few minutes silence Arathea had a brainwave.

'Perhaps we could pretend he is indeed barmy and one of us is his doctor. Carla! You could be convincing as a psychiatrist. In the movies they always have some sort of accent, don't they.'

25

The shout came from the doorway. 'I am Detective-Sergeant Pavel. I have reason to believe that sword is stolen property, sir. Please, everyone stand away from the table.' The newcomer pointed at Kingsley. 'Constable, arrest that man.'

Everyone looked the intruders up and down. The one speaking was about Kingsley's height, in his early thirties, smartly dressed in a dark grey suit. His hair was shiny which made it look blacker than black. The constable who had moved to carry out instructions, was at least as tall as Rogerson, perhaps a little older than me, say twenty-five, with dark-blond hair.

'The young one's handsome, isn't he, Albie?'

'Not to me he isn't.'

'Do you think he'd like to arrest me?'

'He'd never be able to pin anything on you! Ha, ha! Get it?'

'Sadly, yes.'

Carla stepped forward to shield Kingsley. Shoulders straight and dressed in black, she carried authority. 'Not so fast, officer. This man is my patient. I am Doctor Carla Constantinescu. I am a psychiatrist and Mr Kingsley Nutball is in my care.' She stressed the word mister.

He copied her demeanour as he faced up to her. 'I'm sorry madam but—'

'Doctor!' snapped Carla.

Kingsley's mouth opened but no words came.

The policeman continued. 'Doctor, this man has committed a crime and must face charges.' He stood taller as he spoke. It emphasised the crumpled suit.

'Excuse me but I am Doctor Rogerson Lovatt, a colleague psychiatrist of Doctor Constantinescu. Detective, this man is not in his right mind. He lives in an imaginary world.'

'Well, that's as maybe, Doctor but he was caught red-handed stealing that sword and—'

Zinnia joined in. 'We are all psychiatrists; four of the most eminent, not to say expensive, doctors in this field. We are meeting to study this man's special condition. It is called incurable cantankeritis. Due to a slight lapse in security he managed to leave the house. Now he has returned, I assure you he will not escape again.'

'You seem a very conscientious person, Detective,' said Arathea. 'Were you that way in your childhood? How does it make you feel when you arrest someone? Is there a feeling of power over other people? Was this a quality you saw in your father? Or perhaps your mother?'

Trinity and I tittered behind our hands as we watched Kingsley's confused face looking from friend to friend. His head was swivelling enough to twist off, his mouth popping like a fish's.

'Look, er, Doctors, I'm just doing my job. Sorry for any inconvenience but he must come with us. Constable, please hand me the sword and take him away.'

'Not so fast, officer,' said Carla. 'Let me prove to you the state of this man's mind. He has auto-levitation syndrome. He believes objects raise themselves and float in mid-air. Can you imagine how that is for him? Poor soul. I mean, if you saw something like, let me see, that flower vase suddenly rise from the table and float around the room, you would think you were mad, wouldn't you? But now I've said it, that is precisely what poor Mr Nutball will see.'

I took my cue and went to the side table.

'What do you see, Mr Nutball, over there?' Carla said, pointing at me.

The policemen turned in my direction. I raised the vase, trying not to laugh; not that they would have heard me. I walked past the detective, through the table and back again.

'Well, Mr Nutball?' prompted Carla.

'Why are those flowers moving around the room, Dr Carla?'

Next it was Trinity's turn. She picked up the decanter from near the bookcase, carried it and a glass to the octagonal table and poured brandy into a goblet, both appearing to everyone to float in mid-air.

'Thank you very much,' said Kingsley, taking the glass which he promptly emptied and returned to Trinity who carried it away with the decanter.

'Why are you saying thank you?' asked Carla.

'For pouring me a brandy.'

'Ah, of course. I didn't realise I'd done that.'

Kingsley smiled. 'Maybe *you* should see a psychiatrist.'

'Ha, ha. Good joke Mr Nutball. You see what I mean, Detective. None of us saw anything; did you?'

The detective blinked several times as if trying to re-focus his eyes.

The constable looked bemused. 'Um, Sarge—'

I know it's been a long shift. I must be a bit overtired. P'raps if I were a detective sergeant I'd be used to the long hours and double shifts and be able to concentrate. I'm not normally given to seeing things. Not like my dad who's a priest. He's always seeing angels and saints. Went to Lourdes once and swore blind he'd seen St Bernadette. 'Came and had a chat with me as I was eating my cheese roll,' he said. What's that place in Portugal where the little kids saw Mary? Fatima, that's it. Saw a host of angels, he told us when he got home.

I'm fairly sure, though, he's never seen a floating brandy decanter or flower vase. If we weren't on a job, I'd swear it was ghosts. I mean, I don't believe in angels but I do believe in the supernatural. What was that film with Bruce whatsisname? Sixth Sense. Ghosts. It's an old house. Could be they've found a tame spirit and they get it to do tricks for visitors.

Hmn. When we're on our own, I'm going to ask Pavel if he saw it but didn't want to say. Might be detectives' tactics. I've got to learn about those things.

'Quiet, constable. Of course I didn't see anything. But that doesn't change the facts, Doctor. He entered premises unlawfully, removed property unlawfully and attempted to evade the police; also unlawful. On top of that he broke numerous road traffic laws on the way here. Constable, put him in the car.'

Reluctantly, Kingsley allowed himself to be escorted from the room. The detective muttered a few words as he handed a visiting card to Carla.

'Once they get him to the station there's no chance of stopping the process of the law,' said Rogerson.

'Can't you block the drive with your car, darling?' said Arathea.

That gave me an idea.

'Come on, Trinity, quickly! Darling!' I said, grabbing her hand and dragging her to the front door. 'We've got to get on board.' I shouted to the group, 'We'll be back soon.'

The others called after us, 'What are you going to do?' 'Where are you going?'

We raced to the police car parked behind Kingsley's. The constable was having difficulty turning it around; the ground had softened in the rain, giving us just enough time to jump inside. The detective put on a thick outdoor jacket.

'Cold tonight, Ron.'

'Can I quickly pop back for my coat?' Kingsley asked.

'Do you think I was born yesterday? No, you can't!'

I sat next to the driver, Trinity sat between Kingsley and the detective on the back seat.

'What are we going to do?' asked Trinity.

'Is that you, Trinity?' asked Kingsley.

'Be quiet, Nutball!' ordered the detective. 'And the name is Pavel not Trinity.'

'Remember what happened when we tried to stow away on the carriage?'

'Yes, the horse stopped. It was unable to cross the boundary because we were on board.'

'Carriage? Horse?' said Kingsley. 'What are you talking about?'

'I've warned you, Nutball,' said the detective.

'*Doctor* Nutball, if you don't mind.'

'Oh, so you're a doctor too are you? Another trick-cyclist is it? Off your rockers you lot; mad as the patients.'

'And a magistrate!'

'Now I'm quaking in my boots. Just be quiet!'

'Yes, shush, Kingsley,' I said, 'we're trying to get you back to the house.'

'Oh, I see,' said Trinity. 'The car won't be able to get out of the estate and will have to return. Very good, Albie.'

'Only if it works.'

'But if it doesn't, we'll be free.'

'I hadn't thought of that.'

The powerful lights on the front picked out the equipment left for the gardeners who were due the following week. The drive went through what were once sweeping lawns, now ragged scrublands dotted with overgrown, tatty-edged trees, until it became a rough dirt track. Rogerson's vast wealth would return everything to its former beauty. Up ahead I saw the break in the hedgerow signalling the exit from Ruddyard Park. The car slowed on the rutted track as it approached. I crossed my fingers. Our speed dropped even further. We stopped.

The constable did something that made the car whine a lot.

'That means he can't make it go,' said Trinity. 'I remember the American lorries used to do that often.'

'Problem, Ron?'

'Yes, John. Got petrol and battery but it won't restart.'

'Did you two do this?' said Kingsley.

'Sort of,' I replied.

'No, we didn't!' said both policemen.

'I'm not talking to you; I was speaking to Albie.'

The two policemen discussed the situation. The detective used his telephone to speak to someone who made him angry.

'Two hours!' he said to Constable Ron. 'Can't send anyone out for two hours; got a big shout on somewhere. I'm not sitting here for two hours, matey. Come on, back to the house where it's warmer. Alright Dr Nutter, out you get. We're walking.' He picked up the sword and opened the door for Kingsley. 'And don't try anything; I've got the sword don't forget.'

Trinity and I jumped out and hugged each other, happy for the first time we couldn't leave the estate.

'We must hurry back,' she said. 'Kingsley, we're going off to warn the others. Don't run away, it will only cause more trouble. By the time you arrive we'll have a plan. Promise me?'

'Yes, my dear.'

'Oy! Don't you *my dear* me, Nuthead. Call me Detective Pavel if you must talk to me. But I prefer silence.'

'When you were young was it important to have silence in your parents' home?'

'Shut it!'

'Try to get on with him, Kingsley,' whispered Trinity.

The constable stayed in car and tried the engine. It started. Kingsley was quickly pushed back in car. It started to move which caught us out.

'No you don't!' called a gold satin flash.

Trinity flung herself inside through the closed door. The car stopped.

Everyone got out including the driver.

'Nah! It's a goner, sarge.'

'Right, let's go,' said Pavel, yanking Nutball through the open door.

We ran off back towards the lights of the house sparkling through the blackness of the trees' thick foliage. We were puffing a bit by the time we got there.

'Oh!' cried Carla as we rushed through the wall into the drawing room.

She couldn't see me but we'd forgotten she could see Trinity. It must have been a bit disconcerting to see a ghost do that. During the last couple of hours we'd been feeling happy, almost like being alive again, talking to people and included in conversations.

'Trinity! Everyone, Trinity is back. And Albie?'

'Yes, I'm here,' I panted. 'I'll tell you later but we found a way to stop the car. The policemen are walking back here with Kingsley. They can't leave for two hours so we've got a second chance. We need a plan.'

'Do we know where the replica is? Maybe we could find a way of swapping them over and give it to the police. Then convince the police to drop the charges?' suggested Arathea.

'That's even more dishonest than what Kingsley did, darling,' said Rogerson. 'Anyway, we only want the original for about a minute to undo the handle, remove the letter and screw it back. Then they can have it back. I'm not bothered about keeping the original when our copy is perfectly fit for purpose.'

'You're right,' said Zinnia. 'What we need is a distraction to give us time to do what Rogerson said.'

I hadn't realised Trinity was gone until she floated through the door holding the sword. The others saw only floating sword.

'The replica! It was in his car,' she said triumphantly, laying it on the table.

'Ah. Well done, Trinity,' said Rogerson. 'We . . . mightn't need it but it's good to have just in case. So, thank you.'

She beamed. I think she'd taken a liking to Rogerson.

Carla had been busy tapping on a tablet while everyone was talking but now she spoke.

'Yes, I guessed and I was right. I have an idea. We must separate the police so I have Pavel to my own.'

Arathea said, 'I don't mind taking the constable out of the room, if you like. I mean, someone's got to do it.'

That earned her a nudge in the ribs from Rogerson.

Carla spoke again. 'Good. Trinity will be with you. Gather to me. Here is the plan.'

Arathea looked a little sulky as she listened. Having a chaperon wasn't what she had in mind when she volunteered. Her fiancé smiled. We all listened carefully to Carla's proposal.

26

It wasn't long before we heard voices in the entrance hall.

Carla took control and spoke first. 'Ah, Detective Pavel, you have returned Mr Nutball to us. We thank you. Please to sit down.'

'I'm not returning him. Our car has broken down so we had no choice. I need to prevail upon you for a couple of hours until we can be collected.'

'Of course. Please accept my hospitality,' said Rogerson. 'Some fresh coffee has been made, biscuits are on the side and . . .' he winked at the detective, 'there's a little something to take the chill from your bones; we won't tell.'

'Very decent of you, Doctor.' He began to take off his outdoor jacket. Instinctively, I moved to help him then remembered. 'Constable, I think it's safe to let Mr Nutball, or *Doctor* Nutball as he told us he was, haha, sit down. Can you imagine him being a psychiatrist? Mad as a hatter!'

Everyone laughed.

'I wouldn't like to let him treat me,' laughed Zinnia.

'She didn't seem to mind last night,' Trinity whispered to me.

Kingsley sat at the octagonal table where the detective had laid the sword whilst he and the constable wiggled themselves comfortably into two of the easy chairs with their fortified coffees and chocolate biscuits served with fluttering eyelids by Arathea.

'Nice place you've got here, Dr Lovatt.'

'Yes, I'm restoring it with as much of the original furniture and artefacts as I can find.'

This was Arathea's cue. 'That reminds me, we still have a problem in the sitting room. I need a strong man. Constable, would you mind helping me . . . if your superior can release you?'

The detective nodded. Arathea led the other man from the room. Trinity followed. I wished I could be there to watch. Earlier, one of the easy chairs had been prepared by unscrewing three of its four short legs then balancing the chair on top of them. To all appearances it looked perfect but as soon as it was touched it fell over. The policeman's task was to upend the chair and replace the legs. That's where Trinity came into the scheme. As the man was screwing in one leg, she was to unscrew a different one. So, just as he finished one, another fell off. Arathea's task was to keep him at it for as long as possible.

Back in the drawing room Carla was sitting straight backed in the chair adjacent to the other policeman, now on his second, slightly-more fortified, coffee. After his trip into the damp night air his grey suit looked even more scrunched.

She leaned forwards as she spoke in her native language. 'Stii sa vorbesti romaneste?' which she'd told us meant: *Do you speak Romanian?*

'Doar un pic,' he replied.

Carla reverted to English. 'Only a little? Why Jan? Didn't your parents speak it to you?'

'No, they . . . , wait a minute. How did you know I was Romanian? And, more importantly, how did you know my name is Jan? I've always been known as John.'

'Aren't you supposed to be the detective? Pavel? A common Romanian name. I am Constantinescu; another common name. It wasn't hard to work out. Do you remember people of that name?'

'Funnily enough when you introduced yourself I thought it sounded familiar. Where were you from?'

He was hooked, exactly as Carla planned. She glanced at me, flicking her eyes to the side. That was my signal to let Kingsley and Rogerson know they could examine the sword. I went to the table, excitement building.

Rogerson stood with his back to Carla and her fellow countryman. He gripped the scabbard tightly whilst Kingsley twisted the handle. It wasn't budging. He asked Zinnia to help. It wouldn't move. I thought back to Carla's words after the trance.

I said, 'Hold on, Carla said "I turned the handle like this, towards me. I had it in my right hand with the blade in my left."' I mimed as I spoke. He couldn't see me, of course, so I said, 'You're turning it the wrong way.'

'Like this?' whispered Kingsley. 'Here we go. Put your hands on mine Zinnia.'

She didn't need asking a second time. Together they turned as Rogerson held the scabbard. Slowly, slowly the ornate handle unthreaded from the blade until it was free. Kingsley shook it. A rolled-up envelope dropped onto the table. I wanted to grab it and run; find a corner where I could be on my own.

Rogerson flattened out the envelope. The cover was quite clear in its intended recipient: *Mr Daniel Washbury, Ruddyard Park.* I recognised her Ladyship's handwriting.

I had to sit down before I fell. There was a message below in a different script I recognised. It said: *Delivered to Mr D Washbury by Miss E Blessed's hand.*

My Lizzie.

'I feel faint,' I told them.

Kingsley sniggered. 'More than faint, young man, you're completely transparent.'

'Very good, Kingsley,' said Zinnia. 'You have such a wit.'

Normally I would have laughed too but right then I wanted to cry – tears of relief.

'Albie, do you want to open it? Would you like us to leave you alone?' Rogerson spoke gently to me. They all spoke as if they could see me.

'That's kind of you but I'd like to open it when Trinity comes back, if you don't mind.'

'Of course, poor boy,' said Zinnia. 'It's an emotional time.'

I'm sure if she could have seen me, Zinnia would have enfolded me in volumes of garish chiffon.

'Quick, put the handle back; I think Carla's finished with the detective,' said Kingsley.

'I'll go and tell Trinity and Arathea,' I said, rushing off through the closed door, across the hall, and into the sitting room.

There I found Arathea and the constable sitting opposite each other chatting away like old friends. The chair was obviously fixed because he was sitting in it.

'Oh, there you are,' said Trinity, meeting me at the door, a note of disapproval in her speech. She carried on in a soft voice. 'This began as fun but soon became . . . well, just look at them. That woman is such a flirt.'

'I can still hear you, you know,' said Arathea. 'Sorry, Ron, you were saying?'

I was intending to surprise her when we returned to the drawing room but couldn't hold back. 'We've got the letter; it's in the other room.'

'Have you looked?'

'No, I wanted to wait for you, Trinity, so we can see it together.'

'Thank you, Albie.' She pressed her lips to my cheek. 'You are such a sweet man.'

If I could have blushed, I would. 'Carla's finished. They're ready.'

'Come along *Doctor* Arathea,' said Trinity loudly, 'you have to get back to your fiancé!'

'Thank you so much for your help, Ron. We'd better see if your boss needs you. He may want to arrest all of us, you never know,' joked Arathea, taking him by the hand to the door.

Trinity and I didn't bother to wait, we simply took a straight route to the others.

'May want to arrest all of us,' mimicked Trinity. 'Tsk!'

Arathea arrived with Constable Ron in tow and joined the group seated at the table. Rogerson gave her an inquisitive look which she ignored. Carla and the detective were standing nearby, holding hands. I looked twice. Trinity looked twice. Ron frowned and did the same as he took his place next to the detective. Everyone was not only looking at their clasped hands but also their sparkling eyes.

Carla addressed the group. 'It is a strange world, is it not? You know I am Romanian. My part is a small region of Transylvania in the mountains where all the families know each other. Everyone jokes: a few hundred thousand people; only a hundred surnames. And, no Kingsley, none of them are Dracula . . .'

I knew Trinity was back to normal when she muttered, '*None* is treated as singular so one ought to say, *none is*.'

'. . . or Alucard on which the name is said to be based. But, my friends, Pavel, our detective's name, is a common one like my own: Constantinescu. And guess what, we discover we are related, him and me.' She patted his hand. 'Cousins!'

'*He and I*,' mumbled Trinity, 'because—'

'Shush!' I mumbled back.

'But—'

'She's foreign!'

Trinity grunted acceptance of that fact.

'That's amazing!'

'Fantastic!'

'Wow!'

'Hmn, Alucard. I didn't know that.'

Carla continued, 'Jan's family lived in the next valley to ours. We think maybe our grandfathers used to play together as children. I remember my grandmother Cici mentioning the Pavel family. He is cousin on my mother's side, a few times removed. We are family, aren't we, Jan!'

'I propose a toast to that. I could do with a drink,' said Kingsley.

'So could I,' Trinity and I said at same time.

'Purely out of interest, Jan, are you married? Any little Pavels running around anywhere?' asked Zinnia, her green eyes fixed on Carla who glared back with her near-black ones.

Zinnia's weren't the only eyes fixed on Carla. Pavel spoke. 'It's well-known that Romanian men are hard to please so, let's say I haven't found the right . . . dragă românească? Is that the right pronunciation, Carla?'

She grinned. 'Yes, very good, Jan.' She looked at Zinnia. 'He hasn't found the right, um, sweetheart is the simplest translation.' This time Carla's eyes sparkled at Zinnia.

Zinnia looked sceptical at that answer.

I stepped forward, speaking quietly in Kingsley's ear, 'Excuse me, sir, as footman may I have the honour of serving?'

Kingsley smiled. 'Of course, my man.'

What happened next almost caused Jan Pavel's eyes to pop out. I watched, trying to imagine it through his eyes.

A silver tray rises from the side table laden with several brandy goblets and a crystal decanter. It floats across the room to the octagonal table where it comes to rest. The decanter levitates over the tray as each glass is filled with precisely the same quantity of liquid before returning to the table. I always had a good eye for accurate measures. The tray proceeds around the room stopping at each person, ladies first of course, for each one to take a glass before it comes to rest back on the tabletop.

'How . . . ? How . . . ?'

'A party trick of mine,' said Kingsley. 'I just need a little spirit to help me do it. The policemen didn't understand the joke but the doctors hooted. 'Cheers! To families!'

'Familii!' said Carla and Jan as they chinked glasses.

Trinity and I looked on enviously.

'Did you catch that little gleam in her eyes at the mention of a sweetheart?' she said.

Jan cleared his throat ready to speak. 'Can I have your attention, please, everyone. Where Carla and I come from there is a tradition of helping family members, or their friends, in any way. So, Mr Nutball . . . ,' Kingsley opened his mouth to protest at his title but Rogerson poked him in the ribs, '. . . we will return the sword to the rightful owner and consider the matter closed.'

Ron nodded his agreement. 'Good. Case closed.'

'Another toast! To the truly wonderful British Police Force,' called Kingsley.

times. I couldn't remember being so happy in all my life.

A polite cough made us turn.

'Well now, young feller, would you like to untangle from our 'ousemaid and 'ow's about a kiss for the ol' cook,' Mrs Carter laughed as she spoke.

We had a three-way cuddle and a peck for her on each cheek from both of us.

A deeper, more serious cough sounded like a warning cannon. I turned.

I could see his face in my mind's eye. Maybe it was a trick of the memory but he and Kingsley Nutball could be twins.

'So, the wanderer returns,' said Jeremiah Shadwick with no hint of a welcoming smile. 'About your business ladies, if you please.'

'Yes, Mr Shadwick.'

If only I'd known then what I knew later I'd have put my hands around his neck and . . . . Instead I said, politely, 'Good day, Mr Shadwick. I trust you're keeping well.'

He almost sneered. 'No duties for you today, Mr Hapless. Clean yourself up and make sure your uniform is pressed ready for the morning. Supper in the hall as usual. I'm sure the staff would like to hear how her ladyship's new household is progressing. Until then.' He turned and left me standing, staring at the flapping phantoms on the washing lines.

'Hmn. Rogerson could give us his advice, perhaps. But let's see how we feel about it first.'

'You open it then; it's addressed to your fiancé after all.'

Trinity unfolded the sheet of notepaper and we read together:

Mulberry Hall
Cheshire

The nineteenth day of July of the year 1870

Dear Mr Washbury

The bearer of this letter of introduction is one Albert Hapless who was in the employ of Sir George and myself for ten years, latterly as second footman. I hope you will recall my mentioning his name and temporary duties assisting me in Cheshire with the intention he should return to his previous position at Ruddyard Park. I can wholeheartedly praise Hapless as footman, conscientious in all his duties. I must also highly commend his character and bravery in going beyond his everyday responsibilities. If I may, I shall bring to your attention details of the incident which causes my effusiveness.

A matter of months after my arrival at the Hall Albert Hapless was accompanying me on a visit to a jeweller in the nearby town for the purpose of an evaluation of some quite old pieces. I was carrying my jewel case. As I alighted the carriage I was set upon by several footpads. Without troubling you with the details of the ensuing fracas suffice it to say that by the time my trusty footman helped me to my feet, two men lay concussed in the gutter and a third with a bloodied face had been handed over to some local men. Whilst walking me to the front door Albert calmly handed me the case as if it had accidentally fallen from my hand.

I believe he will be an asset to your household, sir.

If I may prevail upon your patience for a moment longer, I have a favour to ask of you. In your employ is one Elizabeth

Blessed, a housemaid, previously serving my household for some five years and always trustworthy and satisfactory in the conduct of her duties. She and Albert Hapless are betrothed and wish to be espoused. It has always been unthinkable, I know, for the lower orders of a household to marry. However, in these enlightened times I wish to ask you to consider allowing the match of two such upright and honest people. Of course, Ruddyard Park is now your domain and the decision is yours to make but I would like to confirm my blessing when Albert puts to you his entreaty.

Whilst writing of perfect betrothals may I ask you to extend my regards to your charming fiancée, Miss Hope, another fine, respectable young person.

I remain, sir, your obedient servant,

Lady Margaret Kingswood

We rested against each other, head to shoulder, and wept, trembling hands clutching shaking bodies. For several minutes we stayed like that. Finally, we parted when Trinity spoke.

'Be careful not to drop tears onto the letter or the ink will run.'

'They're ghost tears, Trinity; they don't touch anything.'

'Of course. For a moment there I'd forgotten I was dead. Thank you so much for reminding me. Anyway, I'm delighted to see Lady Margaret was such an excellent judge of character.'

'Calling me conscientious and brave?'

'No silly, describing me as a fine, respectable young person.'

'We all make mistakes,' I muttered. 'What do you think? Shall we ask the opinion of the others?'

'I do think that. Let's go.'

We marched through several walls, a couple of tables, some chairs, finally arriving in the drawing room. In the dark.

'Oh! Where is everybody?'

'Sitting room?'

We strode off. Nobody there. Nor anywhere on the ground floor.

'I say, Albie, that's a bit of a thing. They've gone to bed! What time is it?'

We were standing in the hall so I checked the grandfather clock.

'Oh dear, it's almost two o'clock on Sunday morning! Perhaps we should go as well and see them in the morning.'

'Alright. Sleep well.'

'I will. What a day.'

Trinity floated up through the ceiling whilst I trudged up the stairs clutching the letter and envelope.

I didn't sleep well. I kept re-living the night I died. It wasn't the being shot; I didn't feel that, nor the wall collapsing on us; I didn't feel that either because I was already dead. No, it wasn't that. I kept seeing and hearing that self-righteous priest pontificating at the Commander, as the policemen called him, when he asked for some compassion for me and Trinity. He had obviously been dead for a long time and I wondered which direction he went in. Do priests automatically go to heaven? If that's where we go and I see him I'll . . . .

"In matters of religion I believe my standing is greater than your own."

Nasty little man. When the Commander told his men he had been tipped off by Father Brimstone, I wondered how a priest would have heard of such a thing. The answer to that question became obvious once I'd found Shadwick's collection of papers.

"Let this be their grave," he said, *"this unconsecrated ground."* As if that wasn't enough, he had to really rub our noses in it. *"I condemn their souls to remain bound to this estate for all eternity – until the Day of Judgement!"*

All this wormed round and round in my head until I was dizzy with anger at the horrid little toad. Eventually I kept coming back to his final words to the Commander.

"If their innocence one day be proved beyond doubt, then the Lord will know and give his blessing."

I wasn't sure if Lady Margaret's letter proved our innocence *"beyond doubt"* but it did show we were good people. I wanted it to be morning. We needed Rogerson's pronouncement as head of the household. Only then, as the priest said, we would be *"welcomed into the Kingdom of Heaven."* No, even better, we'll ask Kingsley; he's a magistrate.

Everyone was slow to rise the following morning, except me and Trinity.

'Bit of an eventful evening for them I suppose,' said Trinity. 'They're all tired out.'

'It was quite eventful for us too but we're here. Do you think the spell or whatever it was will still work?'

We were sitting on the chairs in the hall, waiting.

'Do you mean can they still hear us?'

'I can hear you.' We jumped at Carla's voice behind us. 'And the others should also. But I don't see you. Only a letter floating above the easy chair.'

She was standing in the drawing room doorway holding a tray clinking with last night's glasses. I couldn't put my finger on what it was but, somehow, she looked different; less severe.

'We thought everyone was still in bed,' said Trinity.

'Someone has to clear up. It is my job. You also had a late night?'

'We read the letter,' I said.

'And cried,' Trinity added.

'So, it tells you what you wanted to know?'

'We think so but we need an expert opinion,' I said. I put the envelope on the tray propped between the decanter and a glass. 'Please read it.'

'I am not an expert.'

'Perhaps not but if it weren't for you there would be no letter,' Trinity said with a smile. 'Tell us what you think. Please.'

Carla laid the tray on a side table, sat on the settle, opened the envelope and read. We watched as she wiped the corner of her eye with the edge of her hand.

She held out the envelope for me to take. 'Thank you for letting me. So, who is your expert?'

'Kingsley,' we said together.

'Kingsley! I am surprised. But . . . .'

'He was very brave,' said Trinity.

'And without him we wouldn't have the letter.'

'We thought as he's a magistrate . . . .'

'Yes, this is good reason. I will bring him,' Carla turned, heading for the stairs.

Trinity ran after her. 'Carla! Wait! I . . . I think the doctor may be, um, giving a consultation.

Carla's face lit up as she laughed. 'I know exact what the doctor is giving, young lady. My room is next door.'

'I like her, Albie.'

'Me too. Actually, they're all nice. Even Nutball turned out better than we thought at first.'

An hour or so later with everybody breakfasted we all sat once again at the octagonal table to hear Kingsley's pronouncement. Other than us everyone had a cup of tea or coffee in front of them.

Kingsley cleared his throat. His glasses sat on the table next to his cup. 'OK, here we go,' he said as Trinity and I shuffled in our seats. 'Firstly, as to the case of Elizabeth Blessed. The reason for her attendance in the drawing room on the evening in question is clear from the envelope – delivered by her hand – and the content of the letter contained within. Hardly the action of a criminal, I suggest. If any nefarious dealings were occurring in that room, I don't believe she knew of them and was wrongly charged as being complicit in the crime. I would say Elizabeth Blessed was innocent.'

No-one but Trinity could see my eyes well up. She threw her arms around my neck and kissed me on the cheek as the magistrate continued.

'Next to the matter of Daniel Washbury. He was known to be a solid citizen and fair employer. One city, at least, chose to honour him: the sword. As far as is known he voiced no anti-government opinions and therefore would have no reason to invite a pair of notorious dissenters into his house. There is a strong suggestion the meeting was engineered by the butler.'

'Shadwick!' I sneered.

'From what I've heard,' Kingsley nodded in Trinity's direction, 'I believe Daniel Washbury was set-up and is innocent of plotting murder.'

Now it was my turn to embrace my fellow ghost.

'From what we know, the Secret Police were tipped off by a priest. We must ask ourselves how on earth would a village vicar in the conduct of his normal spiritual duties come to hear of a plot being formulated by two London rogues? I doubt he had ever left village since the day he arrived. I think it most unlikely, don't you?' Everyone nodded agreement.

'So . . . ?' Arathea began.

'Shadwick, the butler – or should we say *fake* butler. It's obvious from his papers he forged his own reference. So, what was he trying to achieve? It is my suggestion he wanted Daniel Washbury out of the way; arrested or dead, he didn't care which, in the belief his weak-willed brother Jacob would take on the house and he, Shadwick, would be able to rule the roost and fiddle enough money on which to retire. Hence the tip-off, and probably a little donation to the church funds, to drop Daniel in the mire.'

'Oh! Oh!' Trinity gasped. 'Albie, I . . . I can't believe he would . . . .'

'For Shadwick, the shooting of Daniel's fiancée and his footman, both of whom he despised, was a bonus. He probably laughed for days at the reverend's condemnation. But his laughter must have died quickly when his plan went awry. Jacob Washbury arrived and sacked everyone.

'Yesss!' said Arathea.

'Silence in court!' joked Kingsley.

'Now we come to the footman and the fiancée. Their character references as given by Lady Margaret Kingswood are impeccable; the two most unlikely people to be involved in any criminal act, let alone a murder plot. And if we accept Daniel Washbury and Elizabeth Blessed were innocent then by implication we must accept Trinity Hope and Albert Hapless are equally so.'

There was absolute silence as Kingsley sat back in his chair with the look of a man who has dispensed justice and good news. He fiddled with his spectacles as he looked around the table.

Arathea was the one who broke the hush with her favourite word.

'Wow!'

She began clapping; a moment later everyone joined in. Including Trinity and me.

'Thank you, Doctor,' I said. 'I wish I could shake your hand.'

'And I wish I could give you a big kiss,' said Trinity.

'I'll do that for you, my dear,' said Zinnia throwing her freckled arms around Kingsley's neck. 'Such a clever man.'

'We can't tell you, Carla, how grateful we are to you . . .' I wished she could see me; I was beaming and grinning from ear to ear. '. . . and to all of you for helping us.' I felt a strange sensation. 'I feel odd,' I said, 'like I'm being pulled away from here. 'Do you feel anything Trinity?'

'Yes, Albie, I do. It's as if someone outside is trying to wrench me away, tugging at my body. I-I think it must be time for us to go. Shall we . . . ?'

28

Behind us I heard Kingsley's voice saying, 'It was nice *not* seeing you! Ha, ha! Good day to be going to Heaven; Sunday.'

With everyone's wishes ringing in our ears we walked through the front door holding hands. Outside was something we'd seen many times when the Americans were here but never believed we'd see our own.

A golden stairway in a shimmering haze. The most beautiful sight I'd ever seen.

'This is it, Trinity, after all this time we're going to see—'

She put her finger on my lips. 'Don't say it out loud; it could be bad luck. Let's just follow the stairs and see where they take us, eh.'

As we climbed, we turned for one last look through the curling mists at Ruddyard Park. The nearby village looked larger but there were still plenty of fields surrounding it. I pointed out the space used each year for the funfair.

Trinity said, 'This is what it must look like from one of those plane machines. Down there. Look. It's the field where we helped the armless army. It's covered in small red-roofed houses.'

'And that's where one crashed,' I said. 'Perhaps we'll meet the man who was flying it.'

'Yes, and all our American friends. How exciting.'

The world below disappeared as we ascended into the clouds. Sometimes the steps appeared translucent like glowing glass, other times they were like solid gold. Even though we were permanently in mist they shimmered as if lit from within by sunlight. The stairway often curved around thick clouds before returning to the straight once more. It was on one of the bends we discovered a golden bench. Next to it was a sign:

> *If the walking hurts your feet,*
> *Stop here and take a seat.*
> *If it's further than you think,*
> *Rest yourself and have a drink.*

We sat.

'If only we could . . . , you know, really have a drink,' said Trinity.

A man dressed in white appeared from a nearby cloud.

'Welcome to The Parrot Eyes Pub.'

'Funny name for a pub, isn't it?' said Trinity.

'Think about it. Did you like my rhyme? What can I get for you madam? Sir?'

We looked at him and each other in amazement.

'Are you being serious?' I asked.

'Of course. Wholly serious. Ha, ha, get it? Holy? Anyway, you can have anything you desire but please don't ask for holy water!'

'Do you serve spirits?' asked Trinity with a straight face.

One Way Street. I investigated *Purgatory Lane*: *Waiting Only. No Exit.*

'For goodness' sake, Trinity, do you want to see Daniel or not? Straight ahead I think,' I said as I jerked her arm to follow.

Much further on we came across more signs. I couldn't read all of them as they seemed to be in different languages but the ones I could make out were *Eden, Elysium, Jannah, Nirvana, Vaikuntha, Valhalla* and finally, *Heaven*.

'No need to say anything. I promise not to be inquisitive. I'll close my eyes, Albie. Take my hand and lead the way, please.'

'Right, here we g . . . . Oh, I get it. *Parrot Eyes*. Sounds like Paradise.'

'Well, I hope the place is better than the jokes.'

I led her along the one path with a familiar name, telling her after a few steps to open her eyes. We began to see colours and shapes through the billows. Here and there the clouds parted so we could see hazy green grass and trees, hedgerows and shrubbery before they closed again.

'It's the Elysian Fields, Albie. We must be almost there. Look! Up ahead!'

In the distance I saw the vague outline of something. Gates. Large. White.

'It's them,' I said as we got closer. 'The Pearly Gates. We've made it.'

'So beautiful.' Trinity stroked the silky-white sheen of the curlicue pattern woven between the bars. 'There's a row of doorbells here, together with a notice.'

We read:

If you are making a delivery, please press one.

If you have tried before to enter but failed, please press two.

If you are lost, please press three.

If you are here for an interview, please press four.

If you believe you have been called too early, please press five.

If you are a new arrival, press six.

If you are a politician, please do not press any bell as you are in the wrong place. Retrace your steps to the first junction.

'Number six is for us,' I said.

'And this must be St Peter . . .' She pointed to a white-robed figure with wings emerging from the cloud next to the gate.

'Y'alright there, boyo?' said the short, pot-bellied man who'd arrived.

'. . . or perhaps not,' mumbled Trinity.

'And what can we do for yous pair, eh?' The Welsh accent was strong.

Trinity started until I kicked her ankle. 'It's not possible to pluralise *you* because—'

'Well, er, we'd like to come in.'

'Would you now? Lorra folk wanna do that, isn't it?'

Trinity turned to me, muttering, 'What did he say?'

I read the man's badge: Gethin. Angel –
Third Rank.

I tugged on the tails of my new white
waistcoat. 'Well Gethin, I suppose we were
expecting to see St Peter, you know, to ask him to
open the gate.'

'St Peter is it?' He tutted several times and
shook his short wings. 'Oh no, no, no. St Peter's
management, see. Pearly Gate Entry Supervisor is a
position assigned by our union only to Angels –
Third Rank like me.' He pointed proudly at his
chest. 'He touches this gate, there'll be a strike
before you can say Land of Our Father.'

Trinity stepped up. 'What is a "our union"?'

Gethin thought the question was hilarious
and took several minutes to stop laughing. 'Where
have you been since 1871?'

'Dead,' we responded.

'What happened? Get lost, did yous?'

'It's a long story. By the way, what's a
strike?'

There was another lengthy bout of hilarity
causing Gethin to have to lean against the gate for
support.

'S'pose you wouldn't know, isn't it. Being
dead and that, like. It's when everyone stops
working but that prob'ly won't happen. More like a
work-to-rule, I'd say. So, Old Pete breaks the rules
by touching these 'ere gates, my guess is union
bosses'll call on us members to work 'em: the rules,
that is. Makes sense, eh?'

'*We* members, not *us*,' Trinity mumbled.

'Not really,' I said, 'but thanks for the explanation. Now Angel – Third Rank Gethin, I'm Footman Albert so I think I out-rank you. Can we see St Peter, please?'

'Where's your chitty then?' He realised from our puzzled expressions his question needed some explanation. 'Bit of paper? The barman should have given it when yous changed into whites. No? He's always doing that. I needs a bit of paper, see. Union rules, isn't it. To protect the Gate Entry Supervisor from any come back, see. You'll have to go on a waiting list. Giz your names, eh?'

I was livid. 'What? We've been on a waiting list for a-hundred-and-fifty-years for G—!'

Gethin put his hand over my mouth. 'Don't say it, pal. For your own good. Trust me, this isn't the place to take His name in vain. Don't go down well, see, considering where you are and that.'

Seeing my anger Trinity took over. 'Our names are Trinity Hope and Albert Hapless.'

'Hold on. I seen them names somewhere.' Gethin reached into a cloud and pulled out a clipboard. He flipped over several leaves of paper each lined with names. He came to an old yellowed one. He stopped and punched the sheet. 'Aha! Wait here!'

He faded into the mist, returning within moments followed by an ancient-looking gentleman with flowing white hair and a white beard which reached almost to his toes. His wings were enormous, the feathers rising from half-way down his legs to an arm's length above his head.

'Welcome both of you. I'm St Peter. Are you really Albert and Trinity?' We nodded. 'We've been waiting such a long time for you, haven't we Gethin?'

'We have that, boss. When I arrived it'd already been over a hundred years. Got my ticket on the picket. Ha, ha, ha. Miners' strike of '84 under St Arthur Scargill.'

'Now, now, young Gethin, you know full well he was not a saint. I might have to report you for that misrepresentation.'

'Oh no, please don't do that Peter. I'll let you open the gate and won't tell the union.'

'We'll see. Anyway, they are a special case so I should be the one welcoming them. As I was saying, so happy to see you. I've been nagged every day for the last hundred-and-forty-odd years by certain people wanting to know if you'd arrived.'

At St Peter's touch the shining pearly-white gates swung open with nothing more than a slight shoosh. The mist on the other side evaporated. He whispered something to Gethin who scurried off through the haze, chest swelling, wings quivering.

'After you,' said the old saint, waving his arm, making me think he'd make a good butler.

Trinity and I stepped ahead through the portal into a clearing, gleaming with silvery light. I sensed the gate swinging behind us. On the far side we saw Gethin approaching with two others, also dressed in white. On his left walked a tall, handsome man with thick brown hair and side whiskers. Even at a distance I could tell he had deep blue eyes. On Gethin's right was a slim, beautiful young woman of medium height. Her long black hair shone reflecting the bright light. Her dark eyes smiled at me.

'Lizzie,' I breathed, voice catching in my throat.

'Daniel. Oh Daniel.'

I felt a hand in the small of my back as St Peter pushed us forward.

And then we four were in the arms of our loved ones, hugging, kissing, weeping, lifting and twirling, whispering names through our tears. The two angels had discreetly disappeared.

My legs were jelly. For the first time in years, my hands were sticky. I felt light-headed. I wanted to sit down. I wanted to dance. I kissed my long-lost love a hundred times. I gazed into her deep eyes, stroked her face, her hair and kissed her another hundred times.

'Oh, Lizzie, my Lizzie. You look so amazing dressed in white – just like a bride.' I dropped to my knee. 'I always believed we were a match made in Heaven. Elizabeth Blessed, will you please do me the honour of being my wife?'

I became aware of Daniel kneeling beside me in front of Trinity.

'Albert Hapless, nothing would make me happier. But I can't marry you now.'

My brain became fogged as thick as the clouds around us. Beside me I heard Trinity catch her breath.

'But, but . . . .'

Lizzie knelt with me, took my face in her hands and kissed me. Then she turned my head and whispered, 'Read.'

On the gate post was a notice.

We regret no
Marriage Services can be
conducted on Sundays.
By order of The Management

Trinity gasped.

As I stared in disbelief, the first three words faded away, changing the meaning entirely.

We regret no
Marriage Services can be
conducted on Sundays.
By order of The Management

A deep, gentle voice boomed, 'Today we can make an exception – or two.'

THE END

ABOUT THE AUTHOR

Maurice Holloway is a British writer living in the west of England. He has written hundreds of short stories and more than twenty novels. He is not tied to any particular genre, choosing instead to write "Whatever I fancy."

He has been writing since 2008 when a friend introduced him to a local writers' group.

When he is not writing, Maurice reads "everything from cereal packets to encyclopedias" as he puts it. He and his wife enjoy travelling to exotic places. In recent years they have visited India, China, the Far East and Mexico. Experiences on these trips frequently find a way into his writing.

Other books by Maurice Holloway

The Favours series (Titus and Jet)
Favour #1 – Steal a Diamond
Favour #2 – Smash the Code
Favour #3 – Hunt the Buddha

Blood on Charing X Road

The Beachcomber
. . . and other stories of the sands

a Diet of Love

KEEP IN TOUCH

Want to find out what other books are in the pipeline?

Subscribe to my newsletter to keep up to date with
forthcoming titles:
https://mauriceholloway.wixsite.com/mauricehollowaybooks

Facebook: https://facebook.com/MauriceHollowayAuthor

Instagram:
https://www.instagram.com/mauricehollowayauthor

Twitter: https://twitter.com/MFHAuthor

Thank you for reading my book. If you enjoyed it, please take
a moment to place a review at your favourite retailer.

Printed in Great Britain
by Amazon